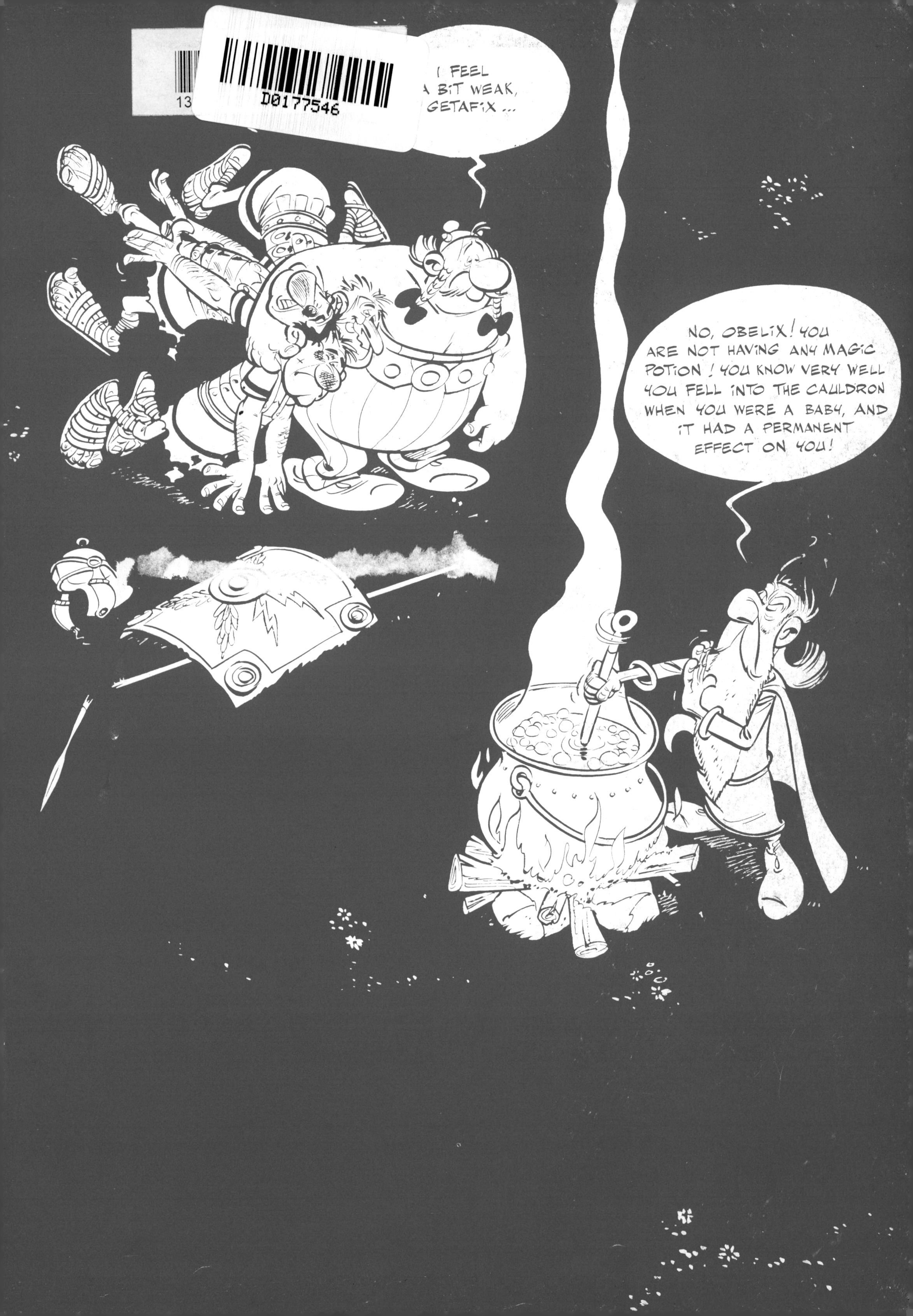
I FEEL A BIT WEAK, GETAFIX ...
NO, OBELIX! YOU ARE NOT HAVING ANY MAGIC POTION! YOU KNOW VERY WELL YOU FELL INTO THE CAULDRON WHEN YOU WERE A BABY, AND IT HAD A PERMANENT EFFECT ON YOU!

GOSCINNY AND UDERZO
PRESENT
An Asterix Adventure

ASTERIX
THE
GLADIATOR

Written by RENÉ GOSCINNY *and Illustrated by* ALBERT UDERZO

Translated by Anthea Bell *and* Derek Hockridge

ORION

Asterix titles available now

1 Asterix the Gaul
2 Asterix and the Golden Sickle
3 Asterix and the Goths
4 Asterix the Gladiator
5 Asterix and the Banquet
6 Asterix and Cleopatra
7 Asterix and the Big Fight
8 Asterix in Britain
9 Asterix and the Normans
10 Asterix the Legionary
11 Asterix and the Chieftain's Shield
12 Asterix at the Olympic Games
13 Asterix and the Cauldron
14 Asterix in Spain
15 Asterix and the Roman Agent
16 Asterix in Switzerland
17 The Mansions of the Gods
18 Asterix and the Laurel Wreath
19 Asterix and the Soothsayer
20 Asterix in Corsica
21 Asterix and Caesar's Gift
22 Asterix and the Great Crossing
23 Obelix and Co.
24 Asterix in Belgium
25 Asterix and the Great Divide
26 Asterix and the Black Gold
27 Asterix and Son
28 Asterix and the Magic Carpet
29 Asterix and the Secret Weapon
30 Asterix and Obelix All at Sea
31 Asterix and the Actress

Asterix and the Class Act

Coming soon

Asterix versus Caesar
The Twelve Tasks of Asterix
Asterix Conquers America
Operation Getafix

Original title: *Astérix Gladiateur*

Exclusive licensee: Orion Publishing Group
Translators: Anthea Bell and Derek Hockridge
Typography: Bryony Newhouse

This revised edition first published in Great Britain by Orion Publishing Group

This hardback edition first published in 2004 by Orion Books Ltd,
Orion House, 5 Upper Saint Martin's Lane, London WC2H 9EA

3 5 7 9 10 8 6 4 2

Printed in France by Partenaires

http://gb.asterix.com
www.orionbooks.co.uk

A CIP record for this book is available from the British Library

ISBN 0 75286 610 9 (cased)
ISBN 0 75286 611 7 (paperback)

Distributed in the United States of America by Sterling Publishing Co. Inc.
387 Park Avenue South, New York, NY 10016

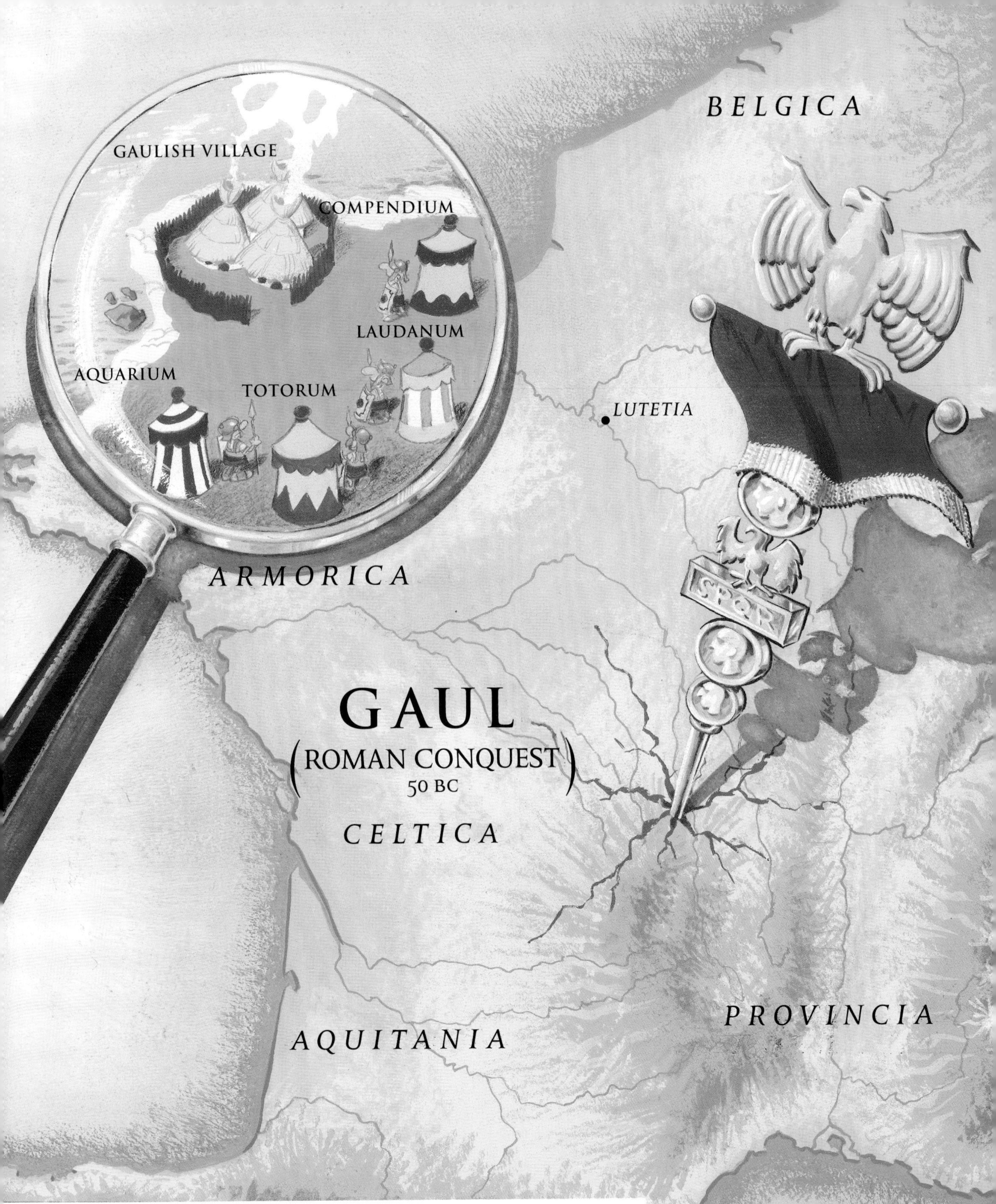
BELGICA
GAULISH VILLAGE
COMPENDIUM
LAUDANUM
AQUARIUM
TOTORUM
LUTETIA
SPQR
ARMORICA
GAUL
(ROMAN CONQUEST
50 BC)
CELTICA
PROVINCIA
AQUITANIA

THE YEAR IS 50 BC. GAUL IS ENTIRELY OCCUPIED BY THE ROMANS. WELL, NOT ENTIRELY ... ONE SMALL VILLAGE OF INDOMITABLE GAULS STILL HOLDS OUT AGAINST THE INVADERS. AND LIFE IS NOT EASY FOR THE ROMAN LEGIONARIES WHO GARRISON THE FORTIFIED CAMPS OF TOTORUM, AQUARIUM, LAUDANUM AND COMPENDIUM ...

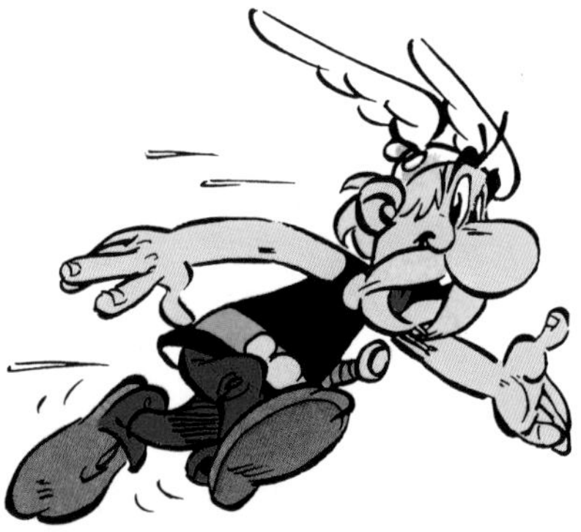

ASTERIX, THE HERO OF THESE ADVENTURES. A SHREWD, CUNNING LITTLE WARRIOR, ALL PERILOUS MISSIONS ARE IMMEDIATELY ENTRUSTED TO HIM. ASTERIX GETS HIS SUPERHUMAN STRENGTH FROM THE MAGIC POTION BREWED BY THE DRUID GETAFIX . . .

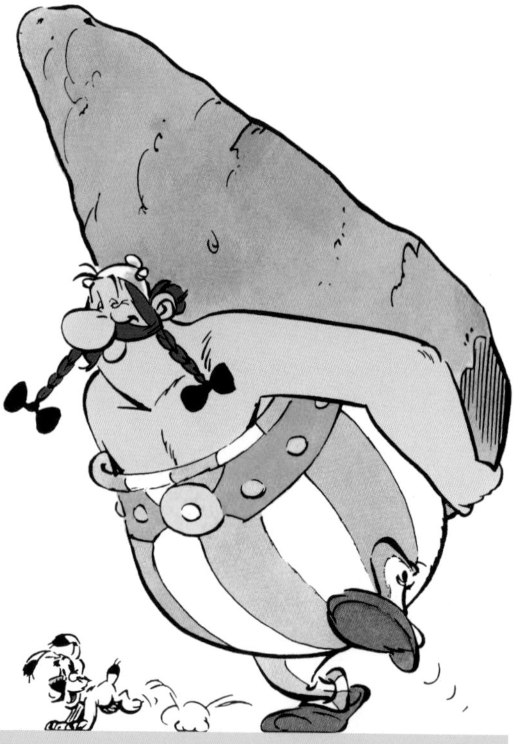

OBELIX, ASTERIX'S INSEPARABLE FRIEND. A MENHIR DELIVERY MAN BY TRADE, ADDICTED TO WILD BOAR. OBELIX IS ALWAYS READY TO DROP EVERYTHING AND GO OFF ON A NEW ADVENTURE WITH ASTERIX – SO LONG AS THERE'S WILD BOAR TO EAT, AND PLENTY OF FIGHTING. HIS CONSTANT COMPANION IS DOGMATIX, THE ONLY KNOWN CANINE ECOLOGIST, WHO HOWLS WITH DESPAIR WHEN A TREE IS CUT DOWN.

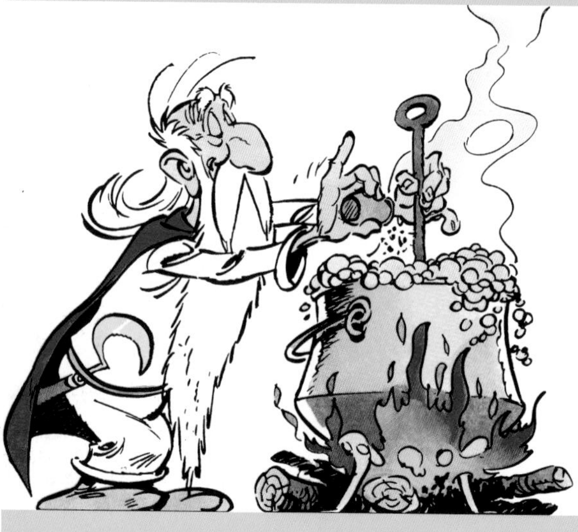

GETAFIX, THE VENERABLE VILLAGE DRUID, GATHERS MISTLETOE AND BREWS MAGIC POTIONS. HIS SPECIALITY IS THE POTION WHICH GIVES THE DRINKER SUPERHUMAN STRENGTH. BUT GETAFIX ALSO HAS OTHER RECIPES UP HIS SLEEVE . . .

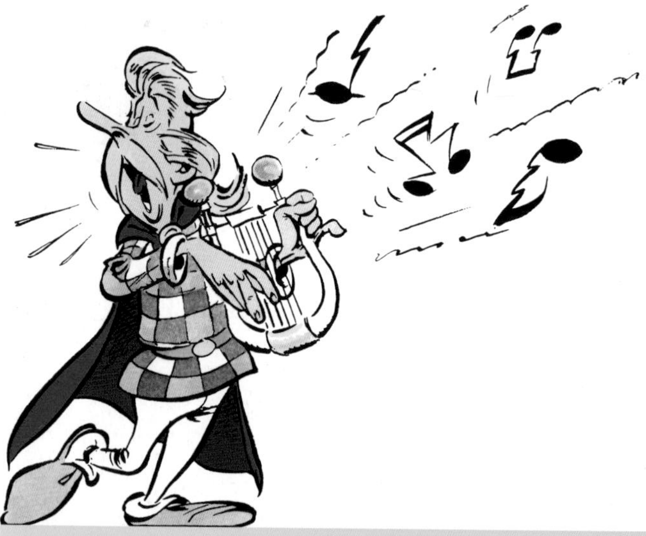

CACOFONIX, THE BARD. OPINION IS DIVIDED AS TO HIS MUSICAL GIFTS. CACOFONIX THINKS HE'S A GENIUS. EVERYONE ELSE THINKS HE'S UNSPEAKABLE. BUT SO LONG AS HE DOESN'T SPEAK, LET ALONE SING, EVERYBODY LIKES HIM . . .

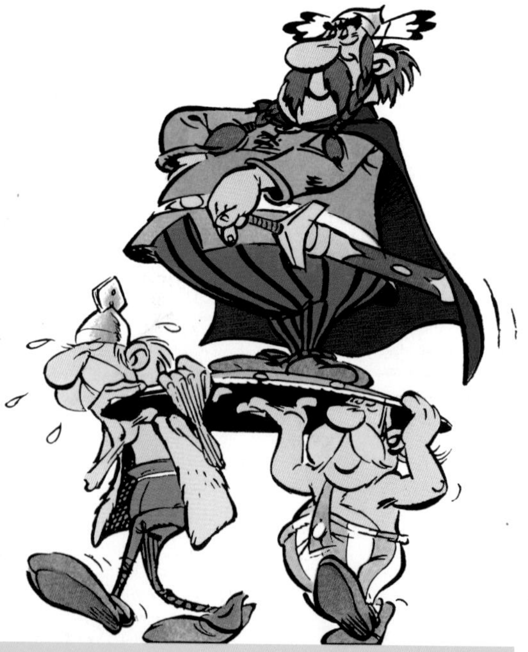

FINALLY, VITALSTATISTIX, THE CHIEF OF THE TRIBE. MAJESTIC, BRAVE AND HOT-TEMPERED, THE OLD WARRIOR IS RESPECTED BY HIS MEN AND FEARED BY HIS ENEMIES. VITALSTATISTIX HIMSELF HAS ONLY ONE FEAR, HE IS AFRAID THE SKY MAY FALL ON HIS HEAD TOMORROW. BUT AS HE ALWAYS SAYS, TOMORROW NEVER COMES.

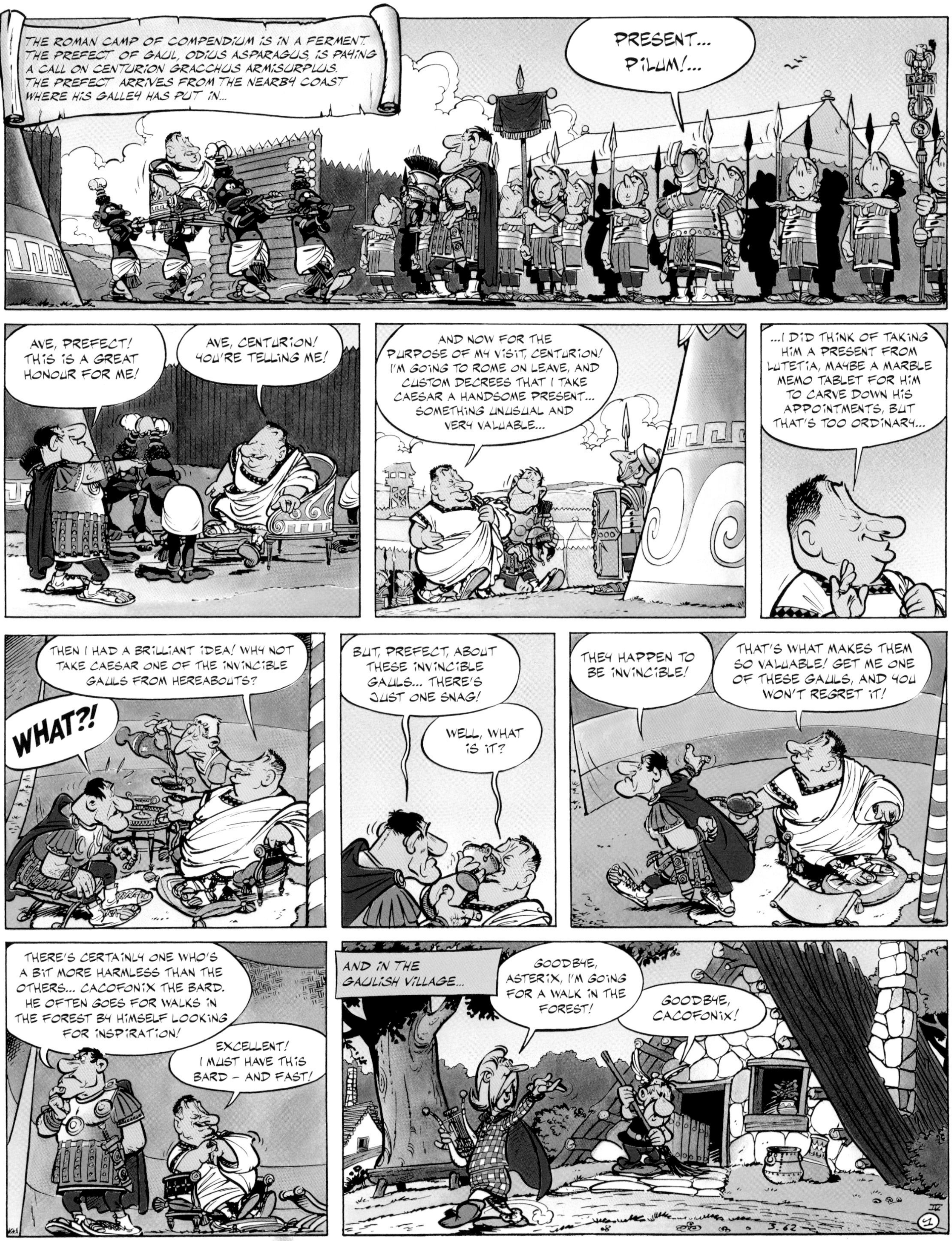
THE ROMAN CAMP OF COMPENDIUM IS IN A FERMENT. THE PREFECT OF GAUL, ODIUS ASPARAGUS, IS PAYING A CALL ON CENTURION GRACCHUS ARMISURPLUS. THE PREFECT ARRIVES FROM THE NEARBY COAST WHERE HIS GALLEY HAS PUT IN...
PRESENT... PILUM!...
AVE, PREFECT! THIS IS A GREAT HONOUR FOR ME!
AVE, CENTURION! YOU'RE TELLING ME!
AND NOW FOR THE PURPOSE OF MY VISIT, CENTURION! I'M GOING TO ROME ON LEAVE, AND CUSTOM DECREES THAT I TAKE CAESAR A HANDSOME PRESENT... SOMETHING UNUSUAL AND VERY VALUABLE...
...I DID THINK OF TAKING HIM A PRESENT FROM LUTETIA, MAYBE A MARBLE MEMO TABLET FOR HIM TO CARVE DOWN HIS APPOINTMENTS, BUT THAT'S TOO ORDINARY...
THEN I HAD A BRILLIANT IDEA! WHY NOT TAKE CAESAR ONE OF THE INVINCIBLE GAULS FROM HEREABOUTS?
WHAT?!
BUT, PREFECT, ABOUT THESE INVINCIBLE GAULS... THERE'S JUST ONE SNAG!
WELL, WHAT IS IT?
THEY HAPPEN TO BE INVINCIBLE!
THAT'S WHAT MAKES THEM SO VALUABLE! GET ME ONE OF THESE GAULS, AND YOU WON'T REGRET IT!
THERE'S CERTAINLY ONE WHO'S A BIT MORE HARMLESS THAN THE OTHERS... CACOFONIX THE BARD. HE OFTEN GOES FOR WALKS IN THE FOREST BY HIMSELF LOOKING FOR INSPIRATION!
EXCELLENT! I MUST HAVE THIS BARD – AND FAST!
AND IN THE GAULISH VILLAGE...
GOODBYE, ASTERIX, I'M GOING FOR A WALK IN THE FOREST!
GOODBYE, CACOFONIX!

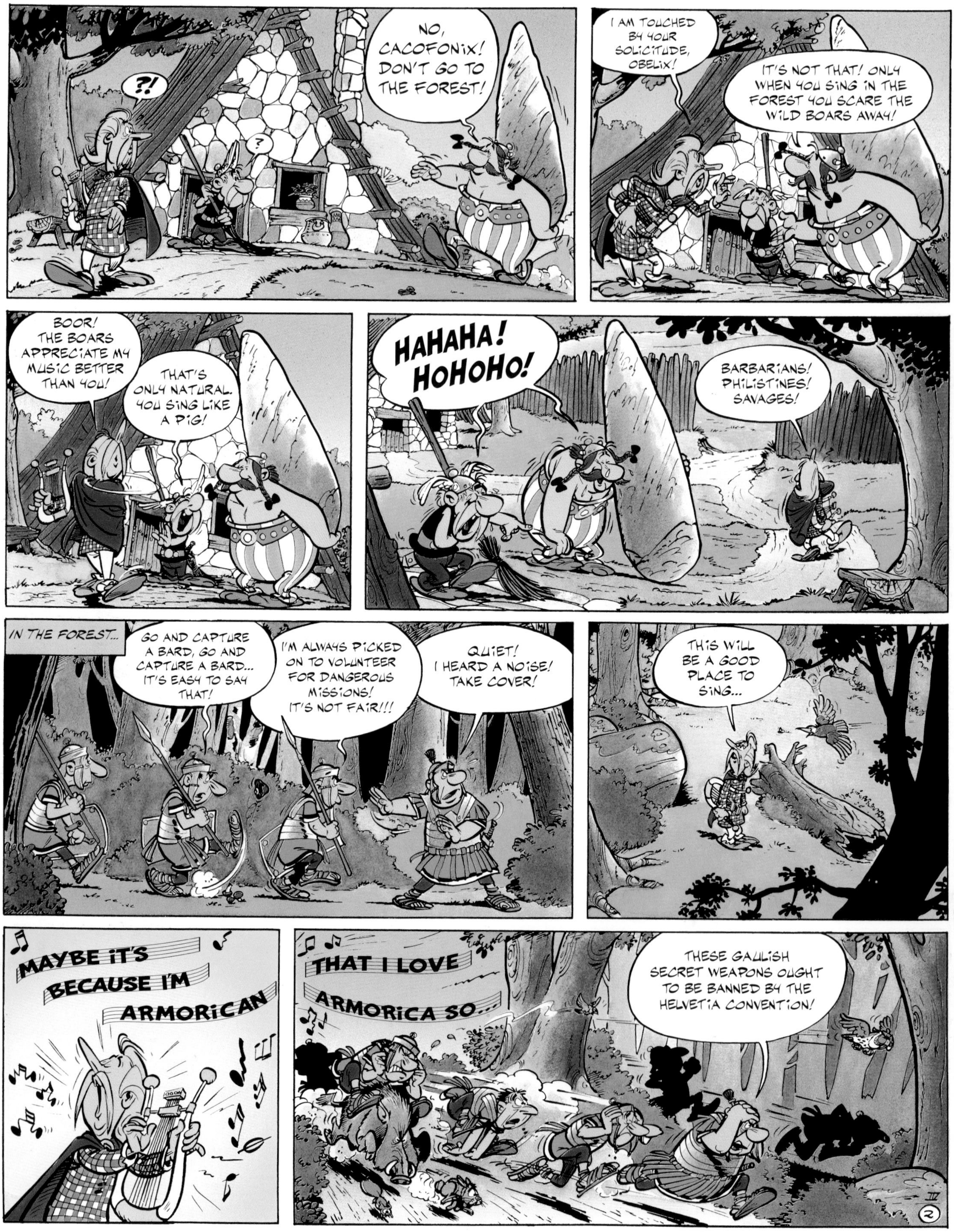
?!
?
NO, CACOFONIX! DON'T GO TO THE FOREST!
I AM TOUCHED BY YOUR SOLICITUDE, OBELIX!
IT'S NOT THAT! ONLY WHEN YOU SING IN THE FOREST YOU SCARE THE WILD BOARS AWAY!
BOOR! THE BOARS APPRECIATE MY MUSIC BETTER THAN YOU!
THAT'S ONLY NATURAL. YOU SING LIKE A PIG!
HAHAHA! HOHOHO!
BARBARIANS! PHILISTINES! SAVAGES!
IN THE FOREST...
GO AND CAPTURE A BARD, GO AND CAPTURE A BARD... IT'S EASY TO SAY THAT!
I'M ALWAYS PICKED ON TO VOLUNTEER FOR DANGEROUS MISSIONS! IT'S NOT FAIR!!!
QUIET! I HEARD A NOISE! TAKE COVER!
THIS WILL BE A GOOD PLACE TO SING...
MAYBE IT'S BECAUSE I'M ARMORICAN
THAT I LOVE ARMORICA SO...
THESE GAULISH SECRET WEAPONS OUGHT TO BE BANNED BY THE HELVETIA CONVENTION!

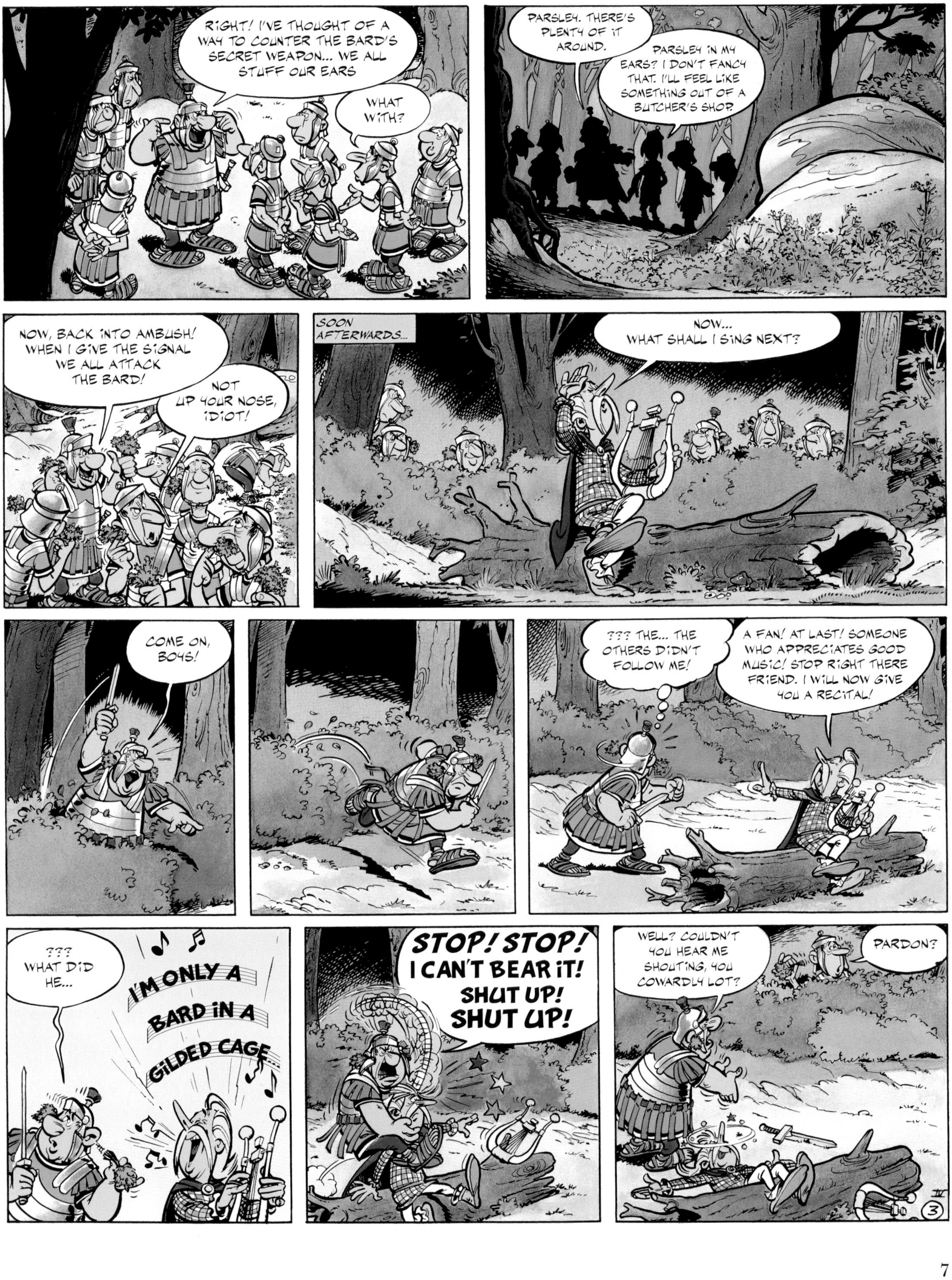
RIGHT! I'VE THOUGHT OF A WAY TO COUNTER THE BARD'S SECRET WEAPON... WE ALL STUFF OUR EARS
WHAT WITH?
PARSLEY. THERE'S PLENTY OF IT AROUND.
PARSLEY IN MY EARS? I DON'T FANCY THAT. I'LL FEEL LIKE SOMETHING OUT OF A BUTCHER'S SHOP?
NOW, BACK INTO AMBUSH! WHEN I GIVE THE SIGNAL WE ALL ATTACK THE BARD!
NOT UP YOUR NOSE, IDIOT!
SOON AFTERWARDS...
NOW... WHAT SHALL I SING NEXT?
COME ON, BOYS!
??? THE... THE OTHERS DIDN'T FOLLOW ME!
A FAN! AT LAST! SOMEONE WHO APPRECIATES GOOD MUSIC! STOP RIGHT THERE FRIEND. I WILL NOW GIVE YOU A RECITAL!
??? WHAT DID HE...
I'M ONLY A BARD IN A GILDED CAGE
STOP! STOP! I CAN'T BEAR IT! SHUT UP! SHUT UP!
WELL? COULDN'T YOU HEAR ME SHOUTING, YOU COWARDLY LOT?
PARDON?
IV
3

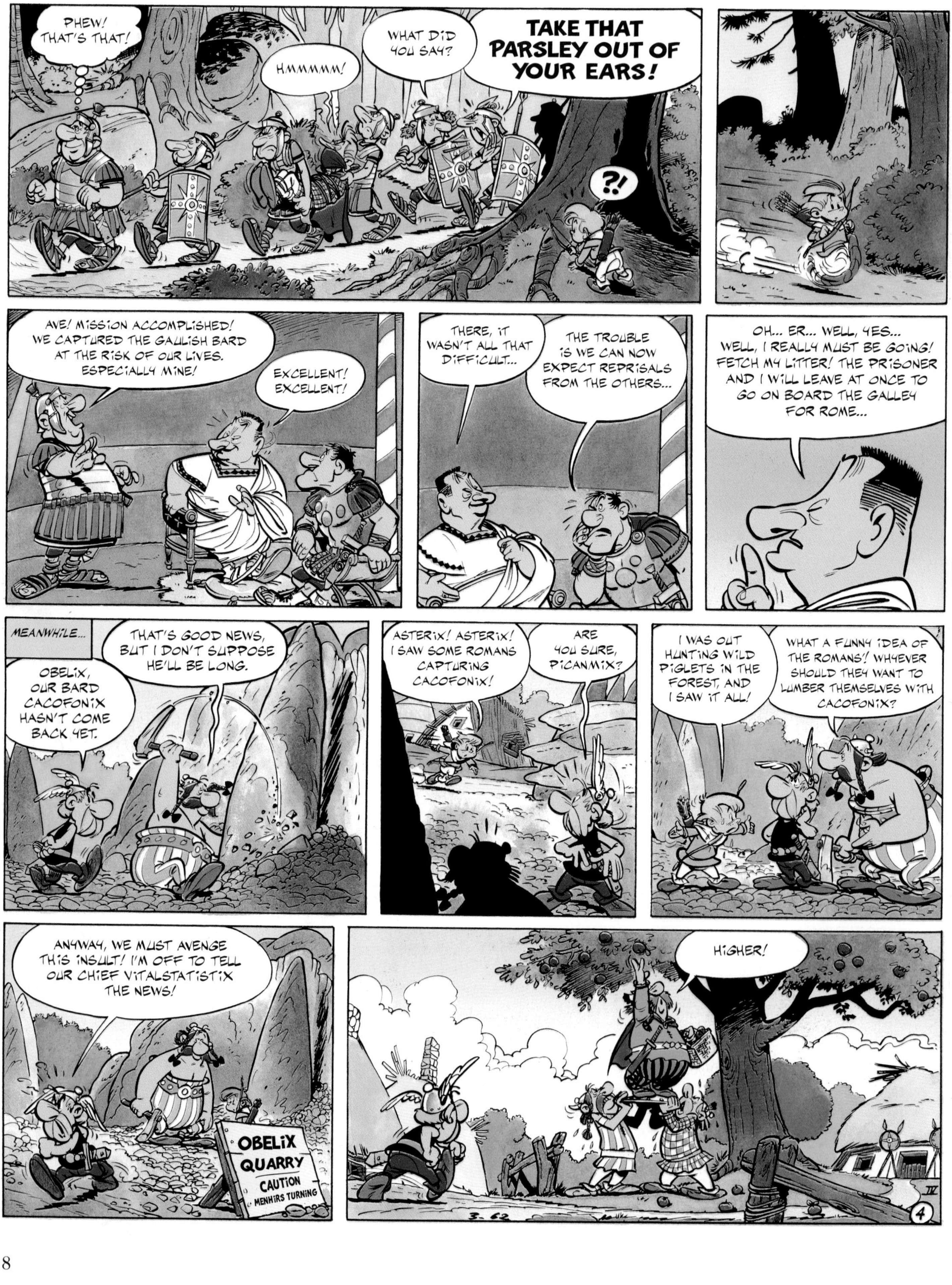
PHEW! THAT'S THAT!
HMMMMM!
WHAT DID YOU SAY?
TAKE THAT PARSLEY OUT OF YOUR EARS!
?!
AVE! MISSION ACCOMPLISHED! WE CAPTURED THE GAULISH BARD AT THE RISK OF OUR LIVES. ESPECIALLY MINE!
EXCELLENT! EXCELLENT!
THERE, IT WASN'T ALL THAT DIFFICULT...
THE TROUBLE IS WE CAN NOW EXPECT REPRISALS FROM THE OTHERS...
OH... ER... WELL, YES... WELL, I REALLY MUST BE GOING! FETCH MY LITTER! THE PRISONER AND I WILL LEAVE AT ONCE TO GO ON BOARD THE GALLEY FOR ROME...
MEANWHILE...
OBELIX, OUR BARD CACOFONIX HASN'T COME BACK YET.
THAT'S GOOD NEWS, BUT I DON'T SUPPOSE HE'LL BE LONG.
ASTERIX! ASTERIX! I SAW SOME ROMANS CAPTURING CACOFONIX!
ARE YOU SURE, PICANMIX?
I WAS OUT HUNTING WILD PIGLETS IN THE FOREST, AND I SAW IT ALL!
WHAT A FUNNY IDEA OF THE ROMANS! WHYEVER SHOULD THEY WANT TO LUMBER THEMSELVES WITH CACOFONIX?
ANYWAY, WE MUST AVENGE THIS INSULT! I'M OFF TO TELL OUR CHIEF VITALSTATISTIX THE NEWS!
OBELIX QUARRY
CAUTION
MENHIRS TURNING
HIGHER!
3. 62
IV
4

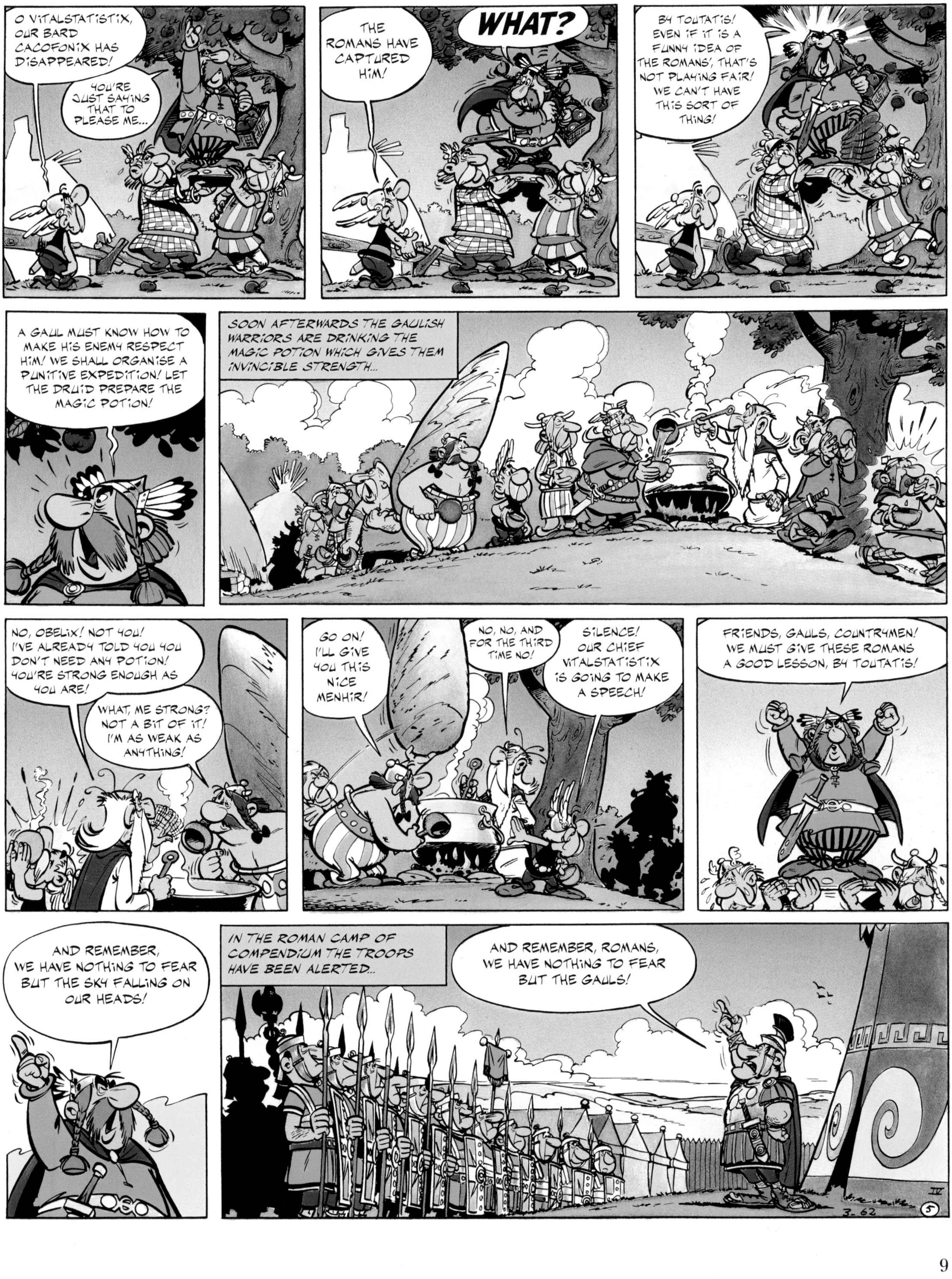
O VITALSTATISTIX, OUR BARD CACOFONIX HAS DISAPPEARED!
YOU'RE JUST SAYING THAT TO PLEASE ME...
THE ROMANS HAVE CAPTURED HIM!
WHAT?
BY TOUTATIS! EVEN IF IT IS A FUNNY IDEA OF THE ROMANS', THAT'S NOT PLAYING FAIR! WE CAN'T HAVE THIS SORT OF THING!
A GAUL MUST KNOW HOW TO MAKE HIS ENEMY RESPECT HIM! WE SHALL ORGANISE A PUNITIVE EXPEDITION! LET THE DRUID PREPARE THE MAGIC POTION!
SOON AFTERWARDS THE GAULISH WARRIORS ARE DRINKING THE MAGIC POTION WHICH GIVES THEM INVINCIBLE STRENGTH...
NO, OBELIX! NOT YOU! I'VE ALREADY TOLD YOU YOU DON'T NEED ANY POTION! YOU'RE STRONG ENOUGH AS YOU ARE!
WHAT, ME STRONG? NOT A BIT OF IT! I'M AS WEAK AS ANYTHING!
GO ON! I'LL GIVE YOU THIS NICE MENHIR!
NO, NO, AND FOR THE THIRD TIME NO!
SILENCE! OUR CHIEF VITALSTATISTIX IS GOING TO MAKE A SPEECH!
FRIENDS, GAULS, COUNTRYMEN! WE MUST GIVE THESE ROMANS A GOOD LESSON, BY TOUTATIS!
AND REMEMBER, WE HAVE NOTHING TO FEAR BUT THE SKY FALLING ON OUR HEADS!
IN THE ROMAN CAMP OF COMPENDIUM THE TROOPS HAVE BEEN ALERTED...
AND REMEMBER, ROMANS, WE HAVE NOTHING TO FEAR BUT THE GAULS!

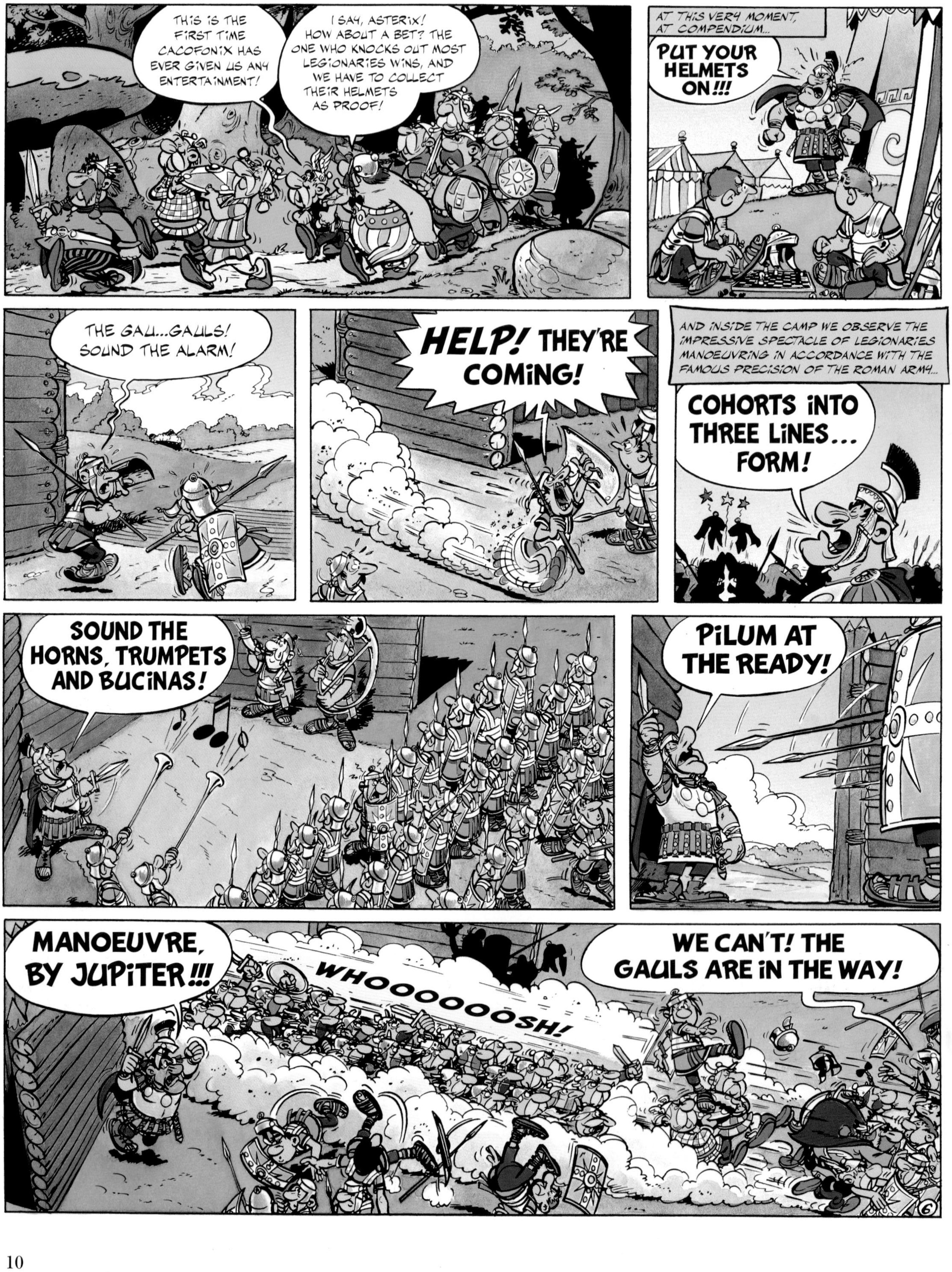
THIS IS THE FIRST TIME CACOFONIX HAS EVER GIVEN US ANY ENTERTAINMENT!
I SAY, ASTERIX! HOW ABOUT A BET? THE ONE WHO KNOCKS OUT MOST LEGIONARIES WINS, AND WE HAVE TO COLLECT THEIR HELMETS AS PROOF!
AT THIS VERY MOMENT, AT COMPENDIUM...
PUT YOUR HELMETS ON!!!
THE GAU...GAULS! SOUND THE ALARM!
HELP! THEY'RE COMING!
AND INSIDE THE CAMP WE OBSERVE THE IMPRESSIVE SPECTACLE OF LEGIONARIES MANOEUVRING IN ACCORDANCE WITH THE FAMOUS PRECISION OF THE ROMAN ARMY...
COHORTS INTO THREE LINES... FORM!
SOUND THE HORNS, TRUMPETS AND BUCINAS!
PILUM AT THE READY!
MANOEUVRE, BY JUPITER!!!
WHOOOOOOOSH!
WE CAN'T! THE GAULS ARE IN THE WAY!
6

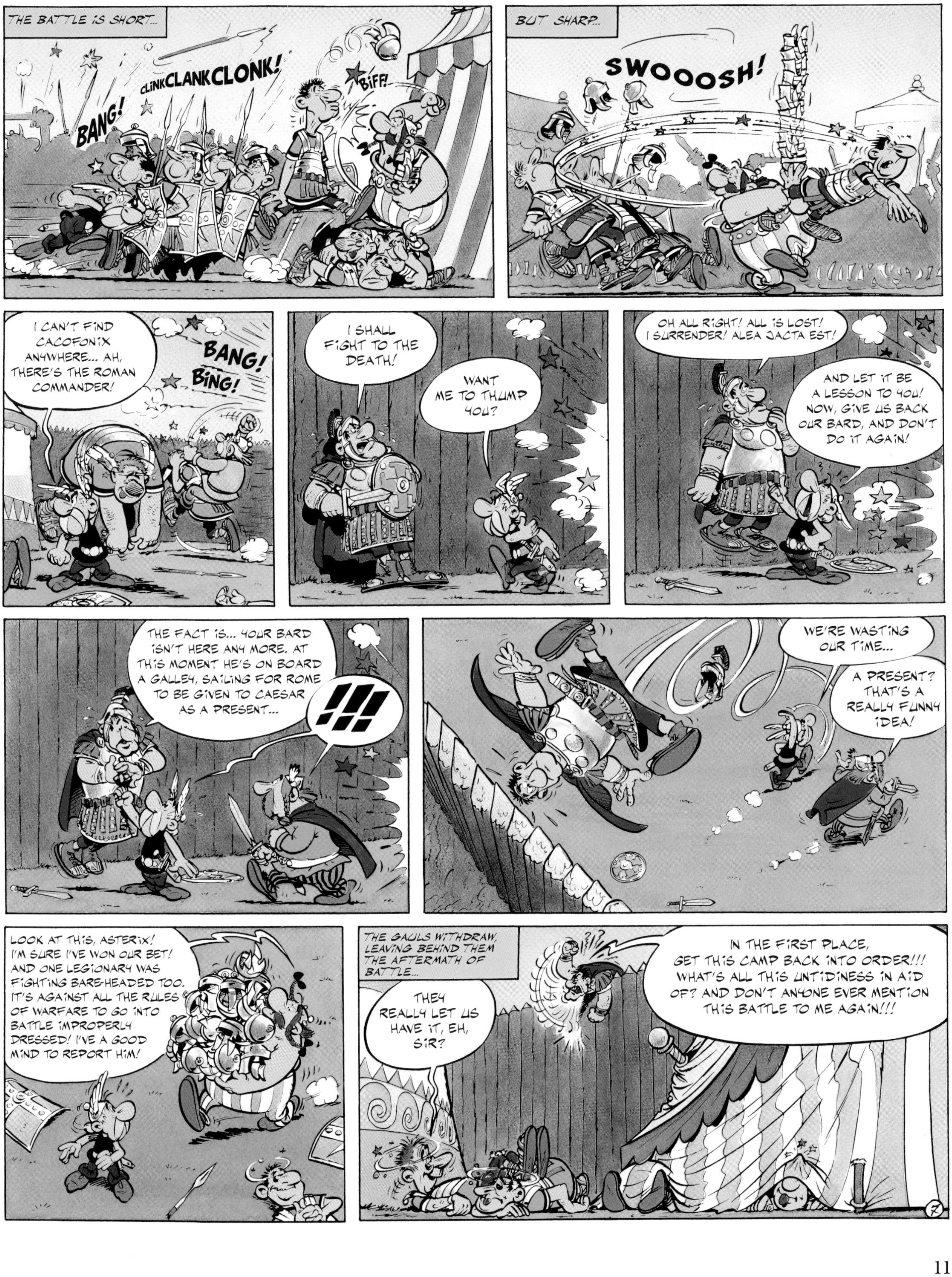
THE BATTLE IS SHORT...
BANG!
CLINK CLANK CLONK!
BIFF!
BUT SHARP...
SWOOOSH!
I CAN'T FIND CACOFONIX ANYWHERE... AH, THERE'S THE ROMAN COMMANDER!
BANG!
BING!
I SHALL FIGHT TO THE DEATH!
WANT ME TO THUMP YOU?
OH ALL RIGHT! ALL IS LOST! I SURRENDER! ALEA JACTA EST!
AND LET IT BE A LESSON TO YOU! NOW, GIVE US BACK OUR BARD, AND DON'T DO IT AGAIN!
THE FACT IS... YOUR BARD ISN'T HERE ANY MORE. AT THIS MOMENT HE'S ON BOARD A GALLEY, SAILING FOR ROME TO BE GIVEN TO CAESAR AS A PRESENT...
!!!
WE'RE WASTING OUR TIME...
A PRESENT? THAT'S A REALLY FUNNY IDEA!
LOOK AT THIS, ASTERIX! I'M SURE I'VE WON OUR BET! AND ONE LEGIONARY WAS FIGHTING BARE-HEADED TOO. IT'S AGAINST ALL THE RULES OF WARFARE TO GO INTO BATTLE IMPROPERLY DRESSED! I'VE A GOOD MIND TO REPORT HIM!
THE GAULS WITHDRAW, LEAVING BEHIND THEM THE AFTERMATH OF BATTLE...
THEY REALLY LET US HAVE IT, EH, SIR?
IN THE FIRST PLACE, GET THIS CAMP BACK INTO ORDER!!! WHAT'S ALL THIS UNTIDINESS IN AID OF? AND DON'T ANYONE EVER MENTION THIS BATTLE TO ME AGAIN!!!
7

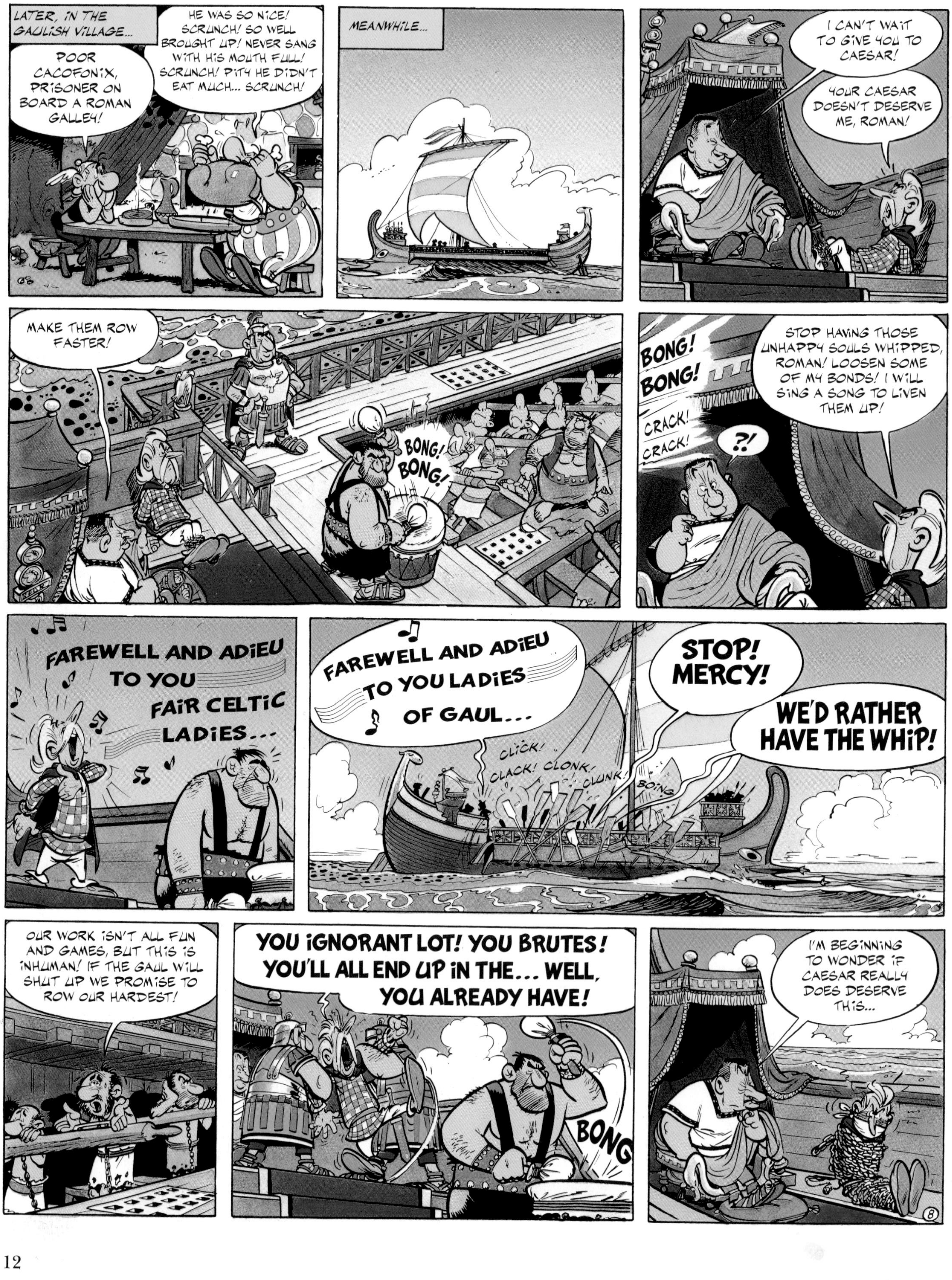

LATER, IN THE GAULISH VILLAGE...
POOR CACOFONIX, PRISONER ON BOARD A ROMAN GALLEY!
HE WAS SO NICE! SCRUNCH! SO WELL BROUGHT UP! NEVER SANG WITH HIS MOUTH FULL! SCRUNCH! PITY HE DIDN'T EAT MUCH... SCRUNCH!
MEANWHILE...
I CAN'T WAIT TO GIVE YOU TO CAESAR!
YOUR CAESAR DOESN'T DESERVE ME, ROMAN!
MAKE THEM ROW FASTER!
BONG! BONG!
BONG! BONG!
CRACK! CRACK!
STOP HAVING THOSE UNHAPPY SOULS WHIPPED, ROMAN! LOOSEN SOME OF MY BONDS! I WILL SING A SONG TO LIVEN THEM UP!
?!
FAREWELL AND ADIEU TO YOU FAIR CELTIC LADIES...
FAREWELL AND ADIEU TO YOU LADIES OF GAUL...
CLICK! CLACK! CLONK! CLUNK! BOING
STOP! MERCY!
WE'D RATHER HAVE THE WHIP!
OUR WORK ISN'T ALL FUN AND GAMES, BUT THIS IS INHUMAN! IF THE GAUL WILL SHUT UP WE PROMISE TO ROW OUR HARDEST!
YOU IGNORANT LOT! YOU BRUTES! YOU'LL ALL END UP IN THE... WELL, YOU ALREADY HAVE!
BONG
I'M BEGINNING TO WONDER IF CAESAR REALLY DOES DESERVE THIS...
8

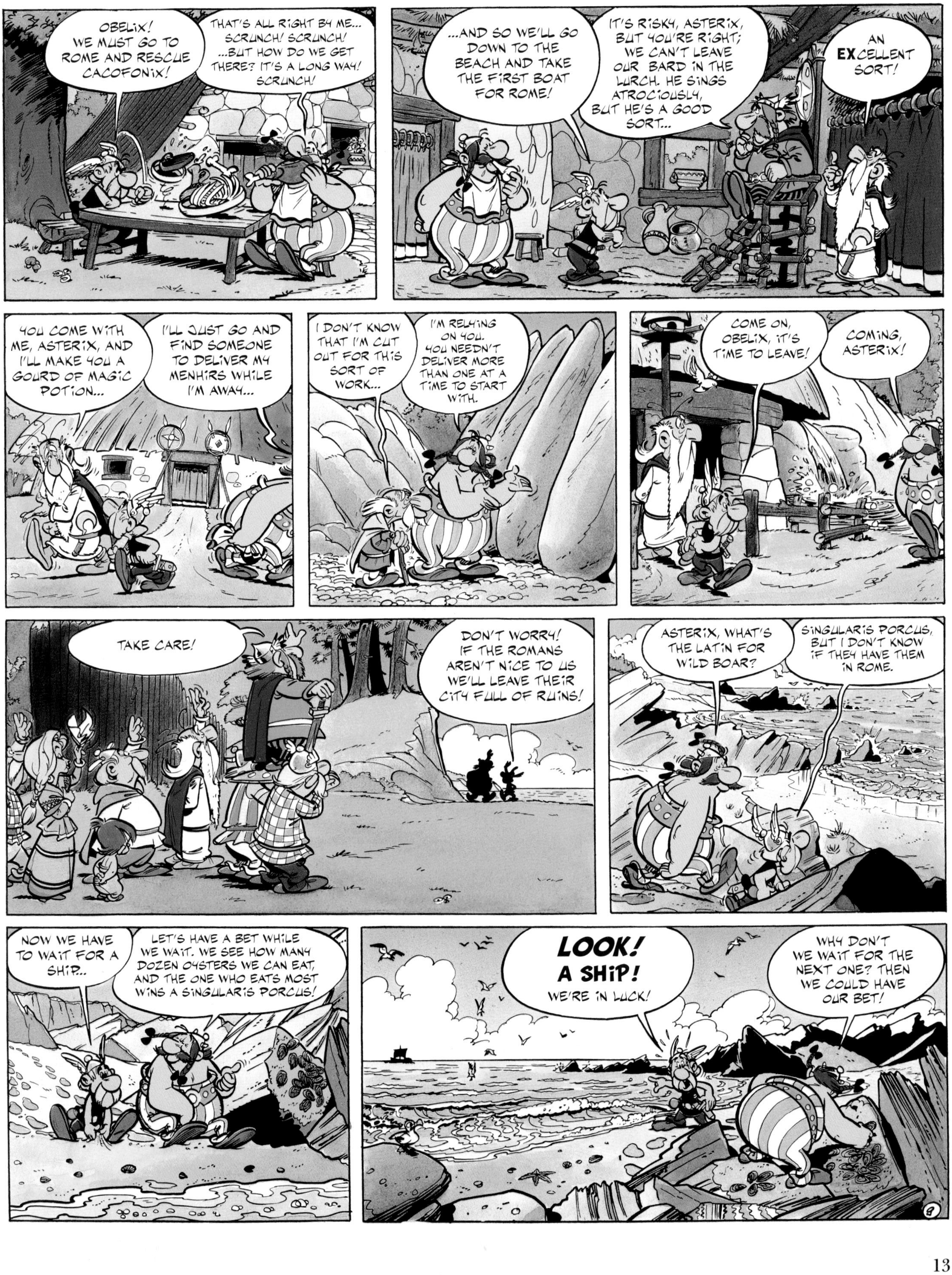
OBELIX! WE MUST GO TO ROME AND RESCUE CACOFONIX!
THAT'S ALL RIGHT BY ME... SCRUNCH! SCRUNCH! ...BUT HOW DO WE GET THERE? IT'S A LONG WAY! SCRUNCH!
...AND SO WE'LL GO DOWN TO THE BEACH AND TAKE THE FIRST BOAT FOR ROME!
IT'S RISKY, ASTERIX, BUT YOU'RE RIGHT; WE CAN'T LEAVE OUR BARD IN THE LURCH. HE SINGS ATROCIOUSLY, BUT HE'S A GOOD SORT...
AN EXCELLENT SORT!
YOU COME WITH ME, ASTERIX, AND I'LL MAKE YOU A GOURD OF MAGIC POTION...
I'LL JUST GO AND FIND SOMEONE TO DELIVER MY MENHIRS WHILE I'M AWAY...
I DON'T KNOW THAT I'M CUT OUT FOR THIS SORT OF WORK...
I'M RELYING ON YOU. YOU NEEDN'T DELIVER MORE THAN ONE AT A TIME TO START WITH.
COME ON, OBELIX, IT'S TIME TO LEAVE!
COMING, ASTERIX!
TAKE CARE!
DON'T WORRY! IF THE ROMANS AREN'T NICE TO US WE'LL LEAVE THEIR CITY FULL OF RUINS!
ASTERIX, WHAT'S THE LATIN FOR WILD BOAR?
SINGULARIS PORCUS, BUT I DON'T KNOW IF THEY HAVE THEM IN ROME.
NOW WE HAVE TO WAIT FOR A SHIP...
LET'S HAVE A BET WHILE WE WAIT. WE SEE HOW MANY DOZEN OYSTERS WE CAN EAT, AND THE ONE WHO EATS MOST WINS A SINGULARIS PORCUS!
LOOK! A SHIP! WE'RE IN LUCK!
WHY DON'T WE WAIT FOR THE NEXT ONE? THEN WE COULD HAVE OUR BET!
8

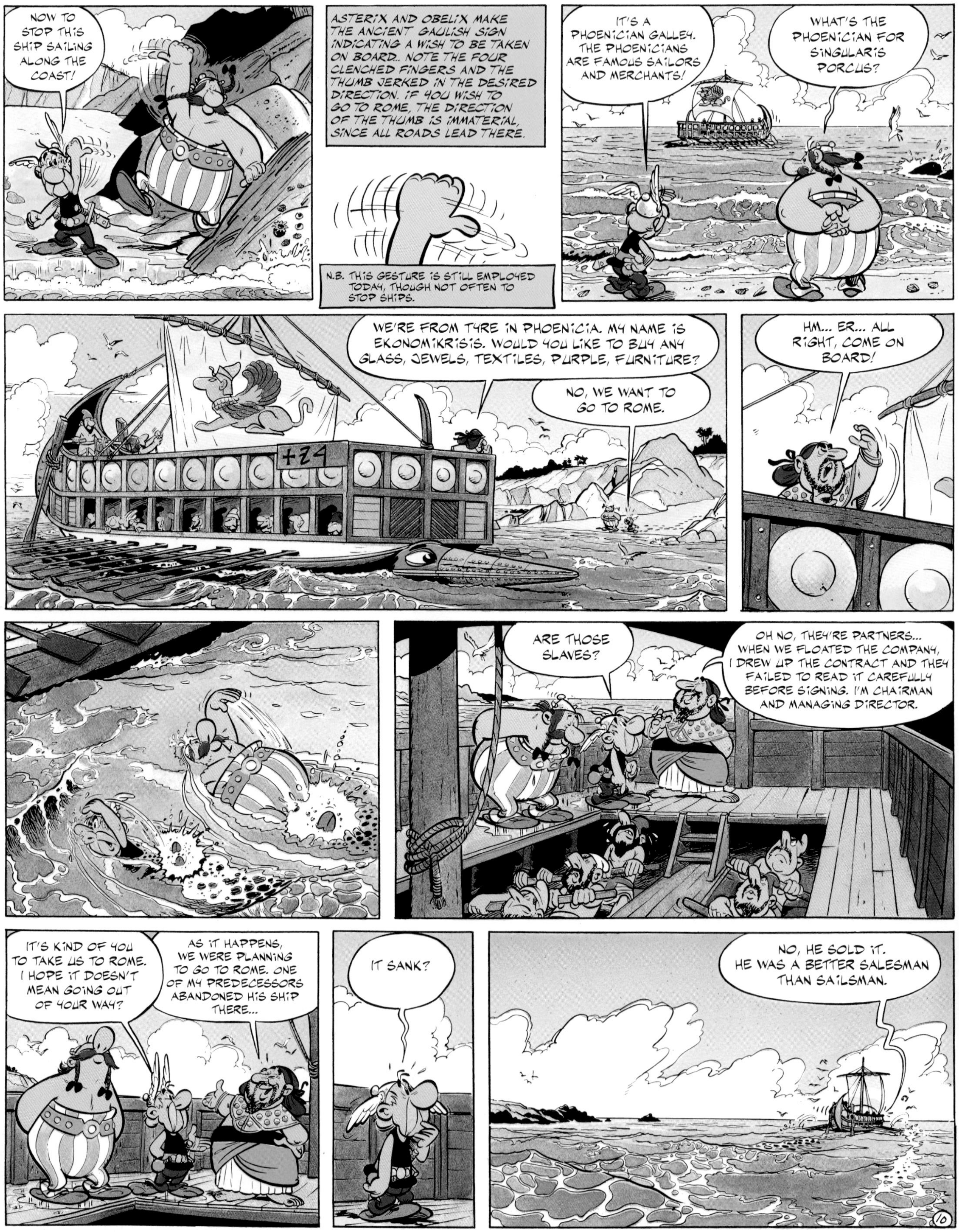
NOW TO STOP THIS SHIP SAILING ALONG THE COAST!
ASTERIX AND OBELIX MAKE THE ANCIENT GAULISH SIGN INDICATING A WISH TO BE TAKEN ON BOARD.. NOTE THE FOUR CLENCHED FINGERS AND THE THUMB JERKED IN THE DESIRED DIRECTION. IF YOU WISH TO GO TO ROME, THE DIRECTION OF THE THUMB IS IMMATERIAL, SINCE ALL ROADS LEAD THERE.
N.B. THIS GESTURE IS STILL EMPLOYED TODAY, THOUGH NOT OFTEN TO STOP SHIPS.
IT'S A PHOENICIAN GALLEY. THE PHOENICIANS ARE FAMOUS SAILORS AND MERCHANTS!
WHAT'S THE PHOENICIAN FOR SINGULARIS PORCUS?
WE'RE FROM TYRE IN PHOENICIA. MY NAME IS EKONOMIKRISIS. WOULD YOU LIKE TO BUY ANY GLASS, JEWELS, TEXTILES, PURPLE, FURNITURE?
NO, WE WANT TO GO TO ROME.
HM... ER... ALL RIGHT, COME ON BOARD!
ARE THOSE SLAVES?
OH NO, THEY'RE PARTNERS... WHEN WE FLOATED THE COMPANY, I DREW UP THE CONTRACT AND THEY FAILED TO READ IT CAREFULLY BEFORE SIGNING. I'M CHAIRMAN AND MANAGING DIRECTOR.
IT'S KIND OF YOU TO TAKE US TO ROME. I HOPE IT DOESN'T MEAN GOING OUT OF YOUR WAY?
AS IT HAPPENS, WE WERE PLANNING TO GO TO ROME. ONE OF MY PREDECESSORS ABANDONED HIS SHIP THERE...
IT SANK?
NO, HE SOLD IT. HE WAS A BETTER SALESMAN THAN SAILSMAN.
10

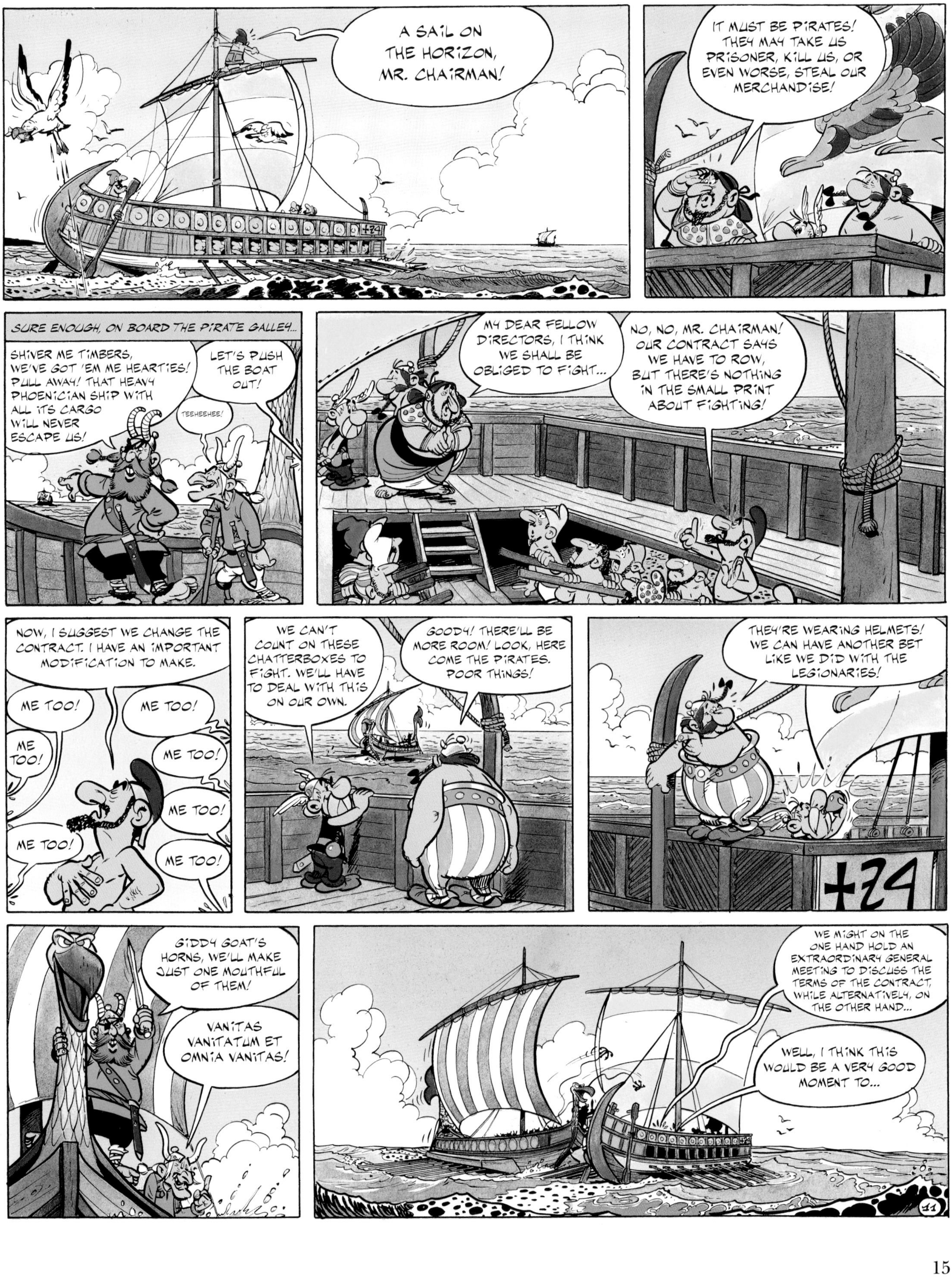
A SAIL ON THE HORIZON, MR. CHAIRMAN!
IT MUST BE PIRATES! THEY MAY TAKE US PRISONER, KILL US, OR EVEN WORSE, STEAL OUR MERCHANDISE!
SURE ENOUGH, ON BOARD THE PIRATE GALLEY...
SHIVER ME TIMBERS, WE'VE GOT 'EM ME HEARTIES! PULL AWAY! THAT HEAVY PHOENICIAN SHIP WITH ALL ITS CARGO WILL NEVER ESCAPE US!
LET'S PUSH THE BOAT OUT!
TEEHEEHEE!
MY DEAR FELLOW DIRECTORS, I THINK WE SHALL BE OBLIGED TO FIGHT...
NO, NO, MR. CHAIRMAN! OUR CONTRACT SAYS WE HAVE TO ROW, BUT THERE'S NOTHING IN THE SMALL PRINT ABOUT FIGHTING!
NOW, I SUGGEST WE CHANGE THE CONTRACT. I HAVE AN IMPORTANT MODIFICATION TO MAKE.
ME TOO!
ME TOO!
ME TOO!
ME TOO!
ME TOO!
ME TOO!
ME TOO!
WE CAN'T COUNT ON THESE CHATTERBOXES TO FIGHT. WE'LL HAVE TO DEAL WITH THIS ON OUR OWN.
GOODY! THERE'LL BE MORE ROOM! LOOK, HERE COME THE PIRATES. POOR THINGS!
THEY'RE WEARING HELMETS! WE CAN HAVE ANOTHER BET LIKE WE DID WITH THE LEGIONARIES!
+24
GIDDY GOAT'S HORNS, WE'LL MAKE JUST ONE MOUTHFUL OF THEM!
VANITAS VANITATUM ET OMNIA VANITAS!
WE MIGHT ON THE ONE HAND HOLD AN EXTRAORDINARY GENERAL MEETING TO DISCUSS THE TERMS OF THE CONTRACT, WHILE ALTERNATIVELY, ON THE OTHER HAND...
WELL, I THINK THIS WOULD BE A VERY GOOD MOMENT TO...
11

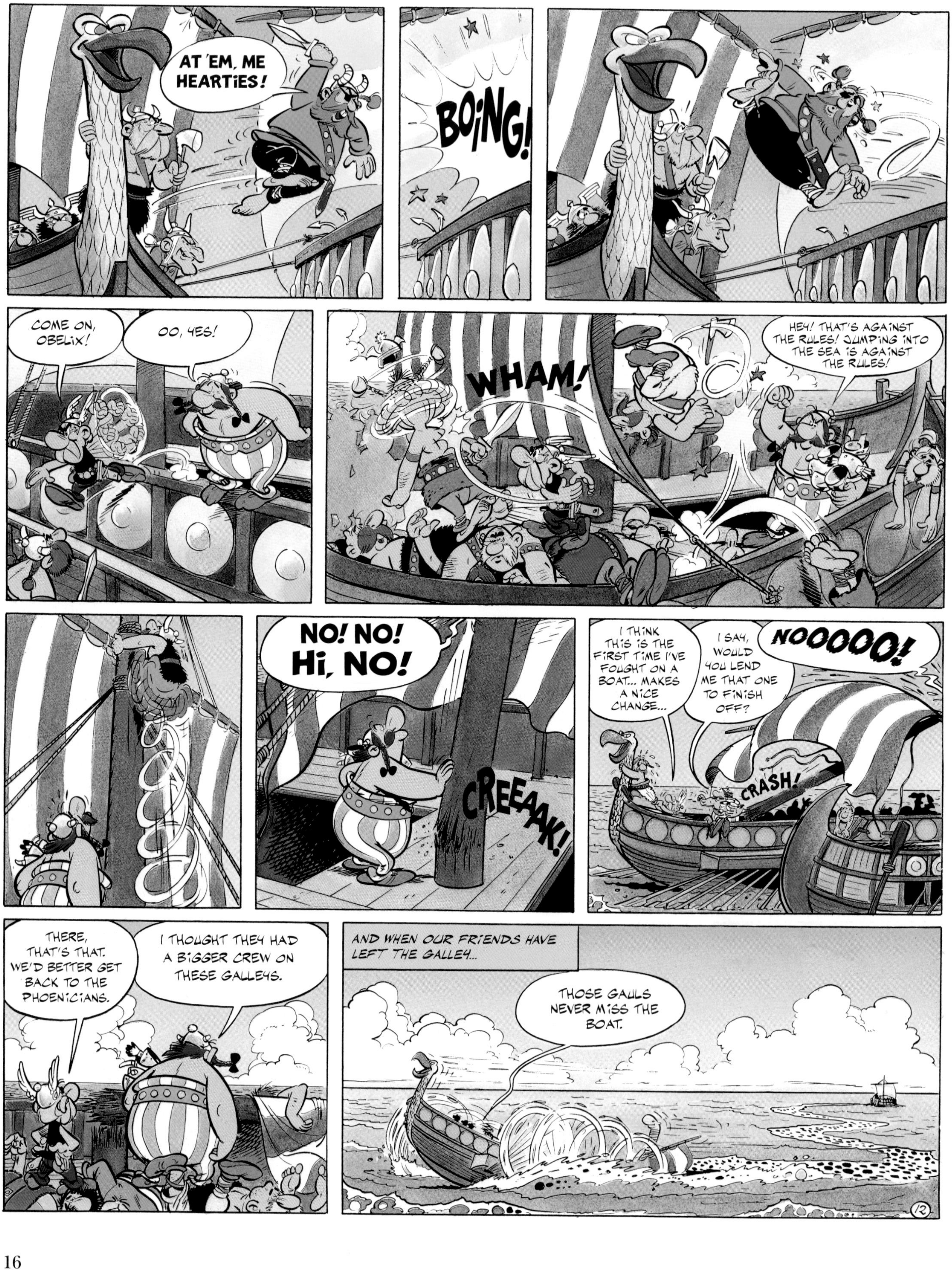
AT 'EM, ME HEARTIES!
BOING!
COME ON, OBELIX!
OO, YES!
WHAM!
HEY! THAT'S AGAINST THE RULES! JUMPING INTO THE SEA IS AGAINST THE RULES!
NO! NO! HI, NO!
CREEAAK!
I THINK THIS IS THE FIRST TIME I'VE FOUGHT ON A BOAT... MAKES A NICE CHANGE...
I SAY, WOULD YOU LEND ME THAT ONE TO FINISH OFF?
NOOOOO!
CRASH!
THERE, THAT'S THAT. WE'D BETTER GET BACK TO THE PHOENICIANS.
I THOUGHT THEY HAD A BIGGER CREW ON THESE GALLEYS.
AND WHEN OUR FRIENDS HAVE LEFT THE GALLEY...
THOSE GAULS NEVER MISS THE BOAT.
12

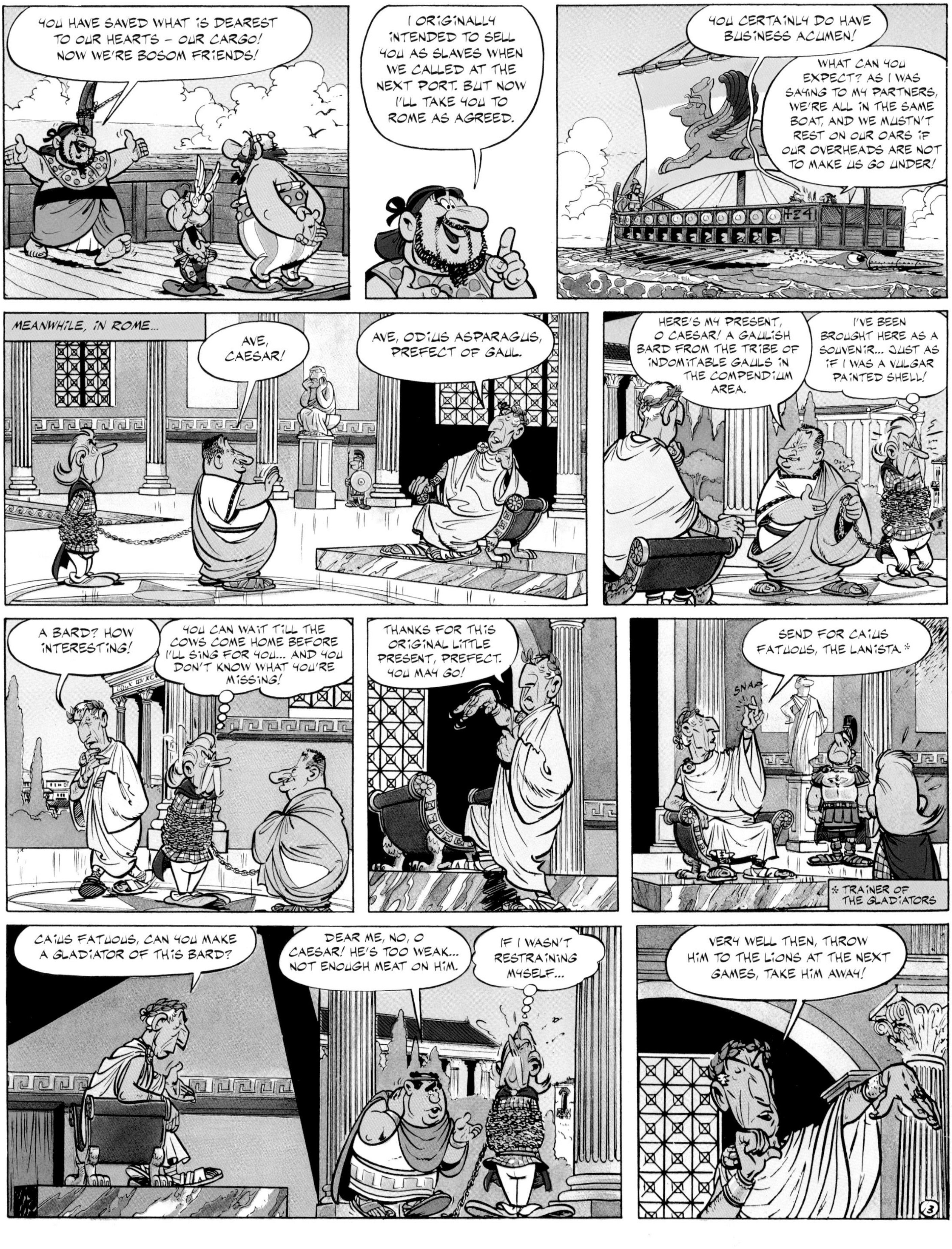
YOU HAVE SAVED WHAT IS DEAREST TO OUR HEARTS – OUR CARGO! NOW WE'RE BOSOM FRIENDS!
I ORIGINALLY INTENDED TO SELL YOU AS SLAVES WHEN WE CALLED AT THE NEXT PORT. BUT NOW I'LL TAKE YOU TO ROME AS AGREED.
YOU CERTAINLY DO HAVE BUSINESS ACUMEN!
WHAT CAN YOU EXPECT? AS I WAS SAYING TO MY PARTNERS, WE'RE ALL IN THE SAME BOAT, AND WE MUSTN'T REST ON OUR OARS IF OUR OVERHEADS ARE NOT TO MAKE US GO UNDER!
MEANWHILE, IN ROME...
AVE, CAESAR!
AVE, ODIUS ASPARAGUS, PREFECT OF GAUL.
HERE'S MY PRESENT, O CAESAR! A GAULISH BARD FROM THE TRIBE OF INDOMITABLE GAULS IN THE COMPENDIUM AREA.
I'VE BEEN BROUGHT HERE AS A SOUVENIR... JUST AS IF I WAS A VULGAR PAINTED SHELL!
A BARD? HOW INTERESTING!
YOU CAN WAIT TILL THE COWS COME HOME BEFORE I'LL SING FOR YOU... AND YOU DON'T KNOW WHAT YOU'RE MISSING!
THANKS FOR THIS ORIGINAL LITTLE PRESENT, PREFECT. YOU MAY GO!
SEND FOR CAIUS FATUOUS, THE LANISTA *
SNAP
* TRAINER OF THE GLADIATORS
CAIUS FATUOUS, CAN YOU MAKE A GLADIATOR OF THIS BARD?
DEAR ME, NO, O CAESAR! HE'S TOO WEAK... NOT ENOUGH MEAT ON HIM.
IF I WASN'T RESTRAINING MYSELF...
VERY WELL THEN, THROW HIM TO THE LIONS AT THE NEXT GAMES, TAKE HIM AWAY!

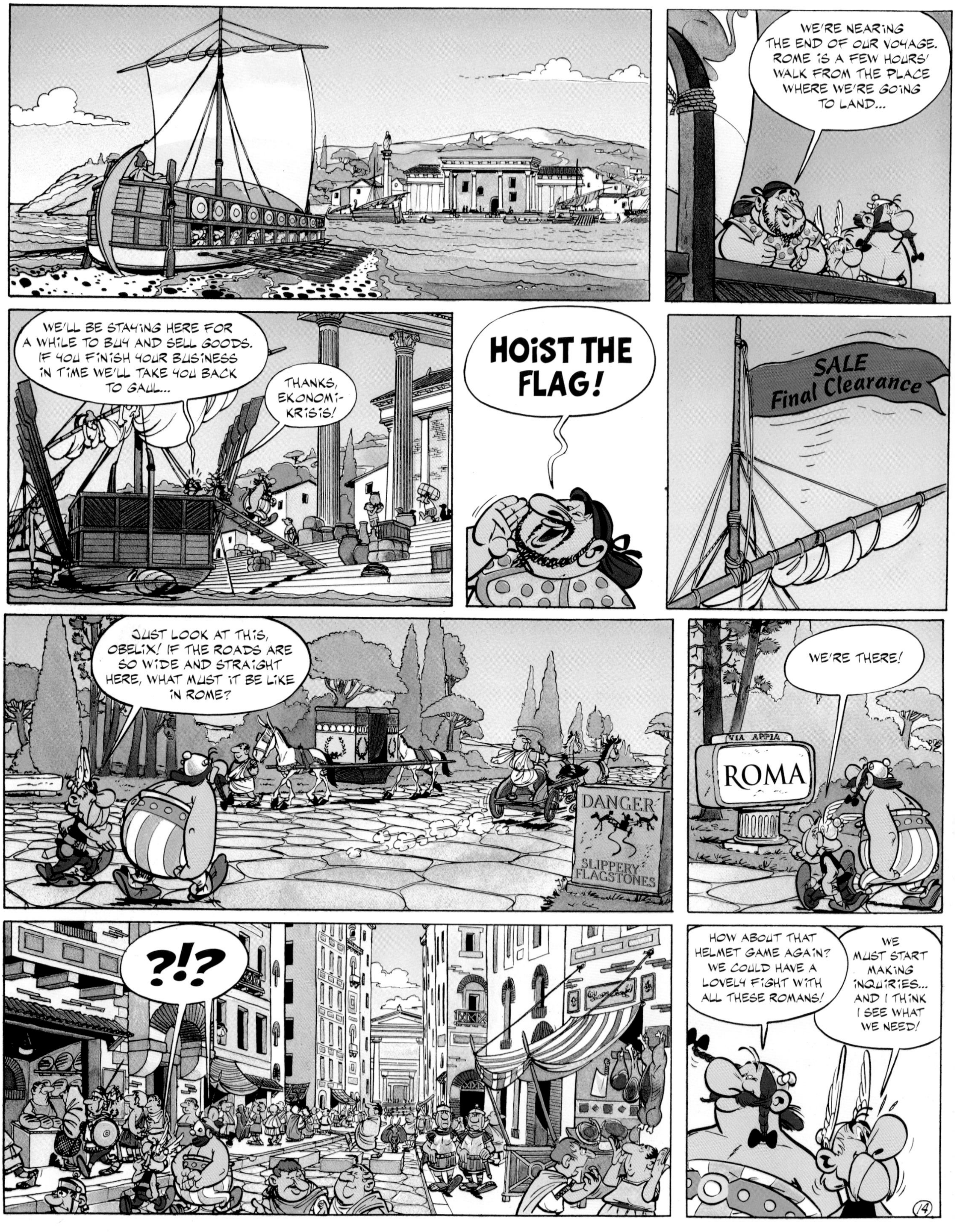
WE'RE NEARING THE END OF OUR VOYAGE. ROME IS A FEW HOURS' WALK FROM THE PLACE WHERE WE'RE GOING TO LAND...
WE'LL BE STAYING HERE FOR A WHILE TO BUY AND SELL GOODS. IF YOU FINISH YOUR BUSINESS IN TIME WE'LL TAKE YOU BACK TO GAUL...
THANKS, EKONOMIKRISIS!
HOIST THE FLAG!
SALE Final Clearance
JUST LOOK AT THIS, OBELIX! IF THE ROADS ARE SO WIDE AND STRAIGHT HERE, WHAT MUST IT BE LIKE IN ROME?
DANGER
SLIPPERY FLAGSTONES
WE'RE THERE!
VIA APPIA
ROMA
?!?
HOW ABOUT THAT HELMET GAME AGAIN? WE COULD HAVE A LOVELY FIGHT WITH ALL THESE ROMANS!
WE MUST START MAKING INQUIRIES... AND I THINK I SEE WHAT WE NEED!
14

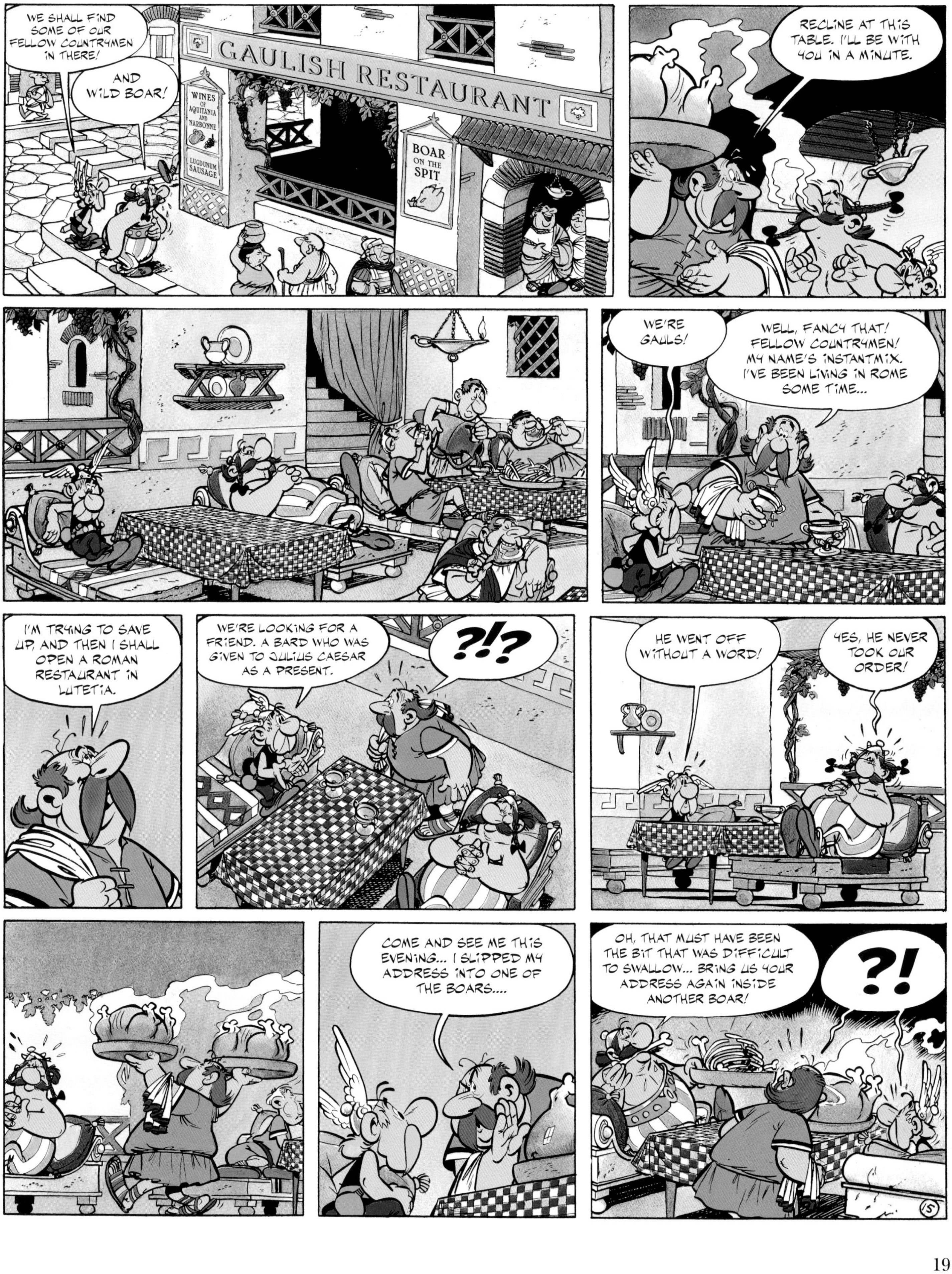
GAULISH RESTAURANT
WE SHALL FIND SOME OF OUR FELLOW COUNTRYMEN IN THERE!
AND WILD BOAR!
WINES OF AQUITANIA AND NARBONNE
LUGDUNUM SAUSAGE
BOAR ON THE SPIT
RECLINE AT THIS TABLE. I'LL BE WITH YOU IN A MINUTE.
WE'RE GAULS!
WELL, FANCY THAT! FELLOW COUNTRYMEN! MY NAME'S INSTANTMIX. I'VE BEEN LIVING IN ROME SOME TIME...
I'M TRYING TO SAVE UP, AND THEN I SHALL OPEN A ROMAN RESTAURANT IN LUTETIA.
WE'RE LOOKING FOR A FRIEND. A BARD WHO WAS GIVEN TO JULIUS CAESAR AS A PRESENT.
?!?
HE WENT OFF WITHOUT A WORD!
YES, HE NEVER TOOK OUR ORDER!
COME AND SEE ME THIS EVENING... I SLIPPED MY ADDRESS INTO ONE OF THE BOARS....
OH, THAT MUST HAVE BEEN THE BIT THAT WAS DIFFICULT TO SWALLOW... BRING US YOUR ADDRESS AGAIN INSIDE ANOTHER BOAR!
?!

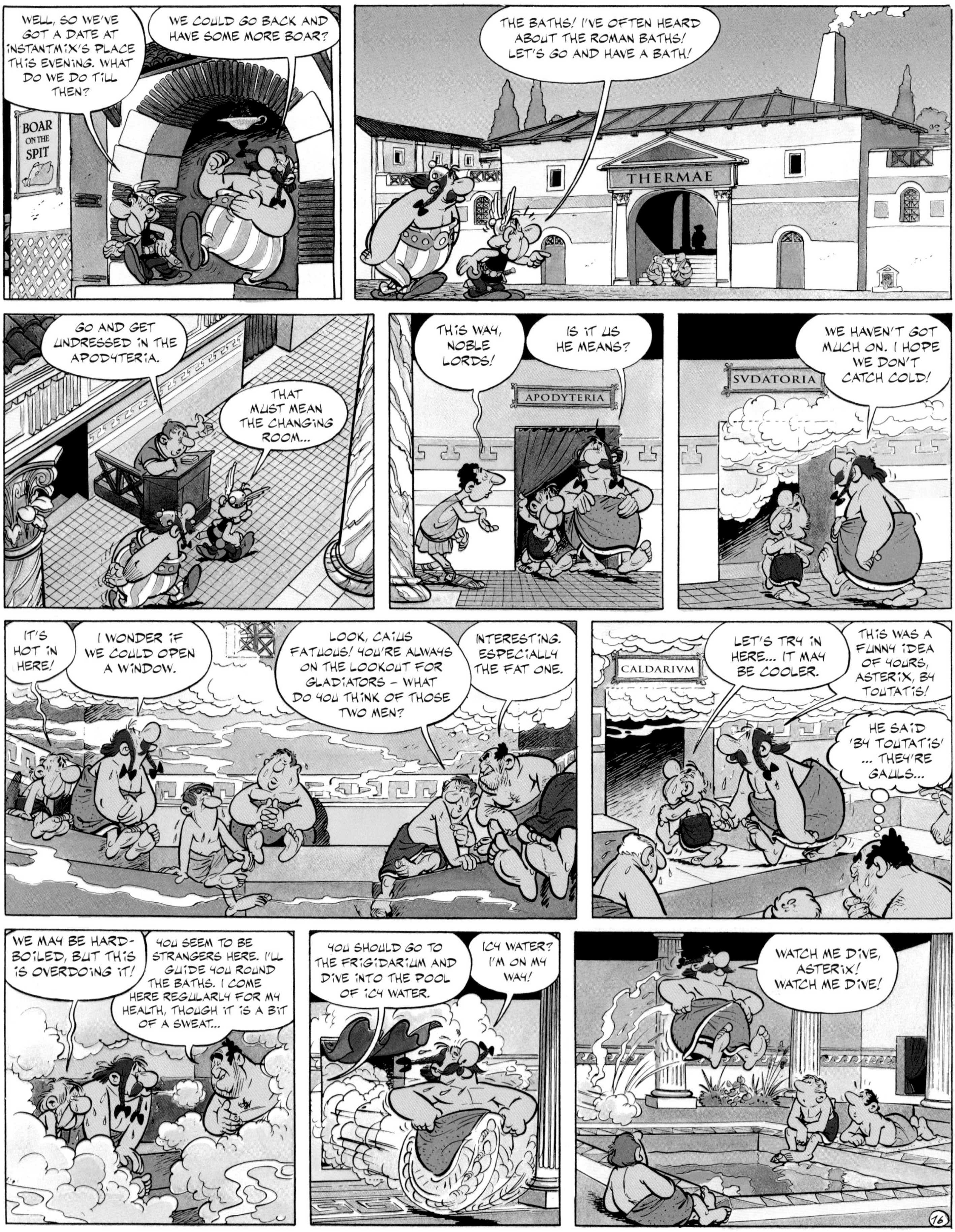
WELL, SO WE'VE GOT A DATE AT INSTANTMIX'S PLACE THIS EVENING. WHAT DO WE DO TILL THEN?
WE COULD GO BACK AND HAVE SOME MORE BOAR?
BOAR ON THE SPIT
THE BATHS! I'VE OFTEN HEARD ABOUT THE ROMAN BATHS! LET'S GO AND HAVE A BATH!
THERMAE
GO AND GET UNDRESSED IN THE APODYTERIA.
THAT MUST MEAN THE CHANGING ROOM...
THIS WAY, NOBLE LORDS!
IS IT US HE MEANS?
APODYTERIA
SVDATORIA
WE HAVEN'T GOT MUCH ON. I HOPE WE DON'T CATCH COLD!
IT'S HOT IN HERE!
I WONDER IF WE COULD OPEN A WINDOW.
LOOK, CAIUS FATUOUS! YOU'RE ALWAYS ON THE LOOKOUT FOR GLADIATORS – WHAT DO YOU THINK OF THOSE TWO MEN?
INTERESTING. ESPECIALLY THE FAT ONE.
CALDARIVM
LET'S TRY IN HERE... IT MAY BE COOLER.
THIS WAS A FUNNY IDEA OF YOURS, ASTERIX, BY TOUTATIS!
HE SAID 'BY TOUTATIS' ... THEY'RE GAULS...
WE MAY BE HARD-BOILED, BUT THIS IS OVERDOING IT!
YOU SEEM TO BE STRANGERS HERE. I'LL GUIDE YOU ROUND THE BATHS. I COME HERE REGULARLY FOR MY HEALTH, THOUGH IT IS A BIT OF A SWEAT...
YOU SHOULD GO TO THE FRIGIDARIUM AND DIVE INTO THE POOL OF ICY WATER.
ICY WATER? I'M ON MY WAY!
WATCH ME DIVE, ASTERIX! WATCH ME DIVE!
16

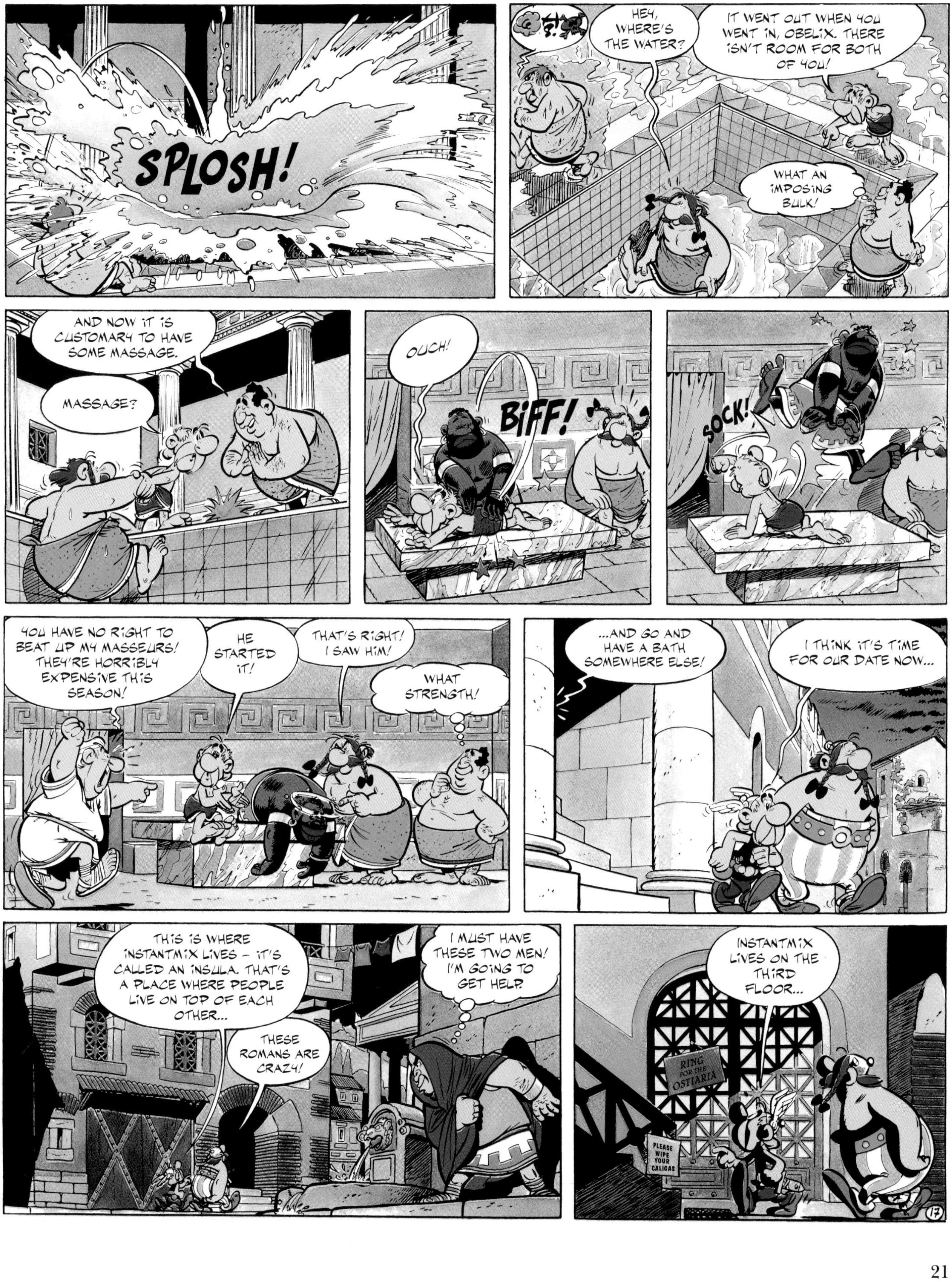
SPLOSH!
HEY, WHERE'S THE WATER?
IT WENT OUT WHEN YOU WENT IN, OBELIX. THERE ISN'T ROOM FOR BOTH OF YOU!
WHAT AN IMPOSING BULK!
AND NOW IT IS CUSTOMARY TO HAVE SOME MASSAGE.
MASSAGE?
OUCH!
BIFF!
SOCK!
YOU HAVE NO RIGHT TO BEAT UP MY MASSEURS! THEY'RE HORRIBLY EXPENSIVE THIS SEASON!
HE STARTED IT!
THAT'S RIGHT! I SAW HIM!
WHAT STRENGTH!
...AND GO AND HAVE A BATH SOMEWHERE ELSE!
I THINK IT'S TIME FOR OUR DATE NOW...
THIS IS WHERE INSTANTMIX LIVES – IT'S CALLED AN INSULA. THAT'S A PLACE WHERE PEOPLE LIVE ON TOP OF EACH OTHER...
THESE ROMANS ARE CRAZY!
I MUST HAVE THESE TWO MEN! I'M GOING TO GET HELP.
INSTANTMIX LIVES ON THE THIRD FLOOR...
RING FOR THE OSTIARIA
PLEASE WIPE YOUR CALIGAS
17

HERE WE ARE ON THE THIRD FLOOR...

THESE ROMANS ARE CRAZY!

STOP WASTING TIME AND KNOCK AT THIS DOOR!

RIGHT!

CRASH!

I SAID KNOCK! I DIDN'T SAY SMASH IT IN!

DON'T SHOUT AT ME! YOU KNOW KNOCKING AND SMASHING COME TO THE SAME THING WITH ME!

WHAT'S ALL THIS?

ER... DOES INSTANTMIX LIVE HERE?

I'LL JUST KNOCK...

NO! HE LIVES OPPOSITE!

CRASH!

DON'T TOUCH ANY MORE DOORS!

YOU KEEP ON SHOUTING! I DIDN'T SHOUT AT YOU WHEN YOU GOT US INTO HOT WATER JUST NOW, DID I?

WHAT ABOUT MY DOOR? YOU THINK YOU CAN GET AWAY WITH THIS?

LET'S HAVE A BIT OF PEACE! WE'RE TRYING TO SLEEP, BY JUPITER!

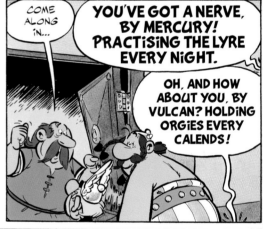

COME ALONG IN...

YOU'VE GOT A NERVE, BY MERCURY! PRACTISING THE LYRE EVERY NIGHT.

OH, AND HOW ABOUT YOU, BY VULCAN? HOLDING ORGIES EVERY CALENDS!

NICE PLACE YOU'VE GOT HERE....

OH, IT'S JUST A SMALL FLAT – CUBICULUM, KITCHEN, TRICLINIUM, AND YOU HAVE TO GO DOWN TO THE AQUEDUCT FOR WATER...

AND WHAT DO YOU CALL THIS SORT OF PLACE?

OH, THESE ARE GLC FLATS – GREATER LATIN COUNCIL...

18

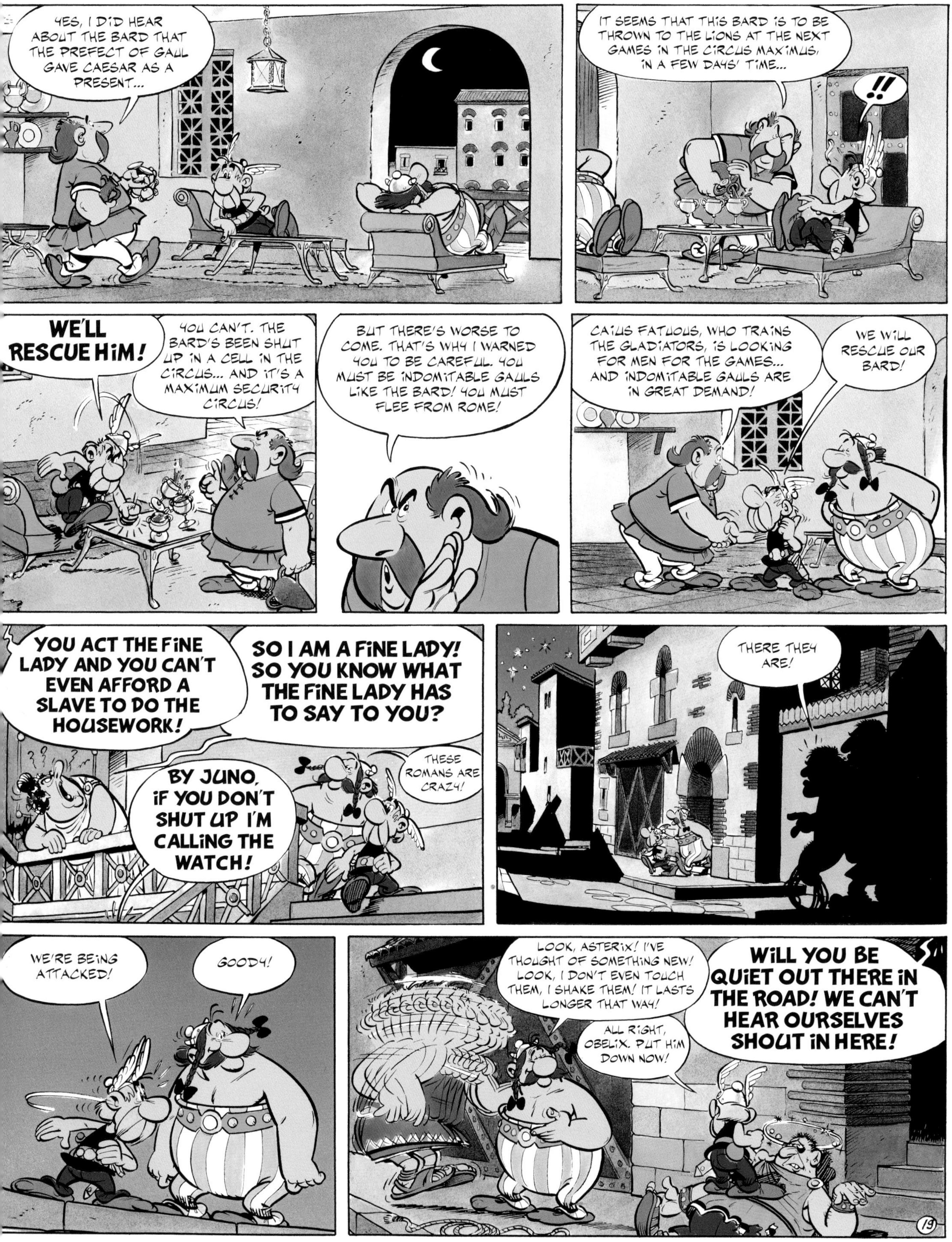

YES, I DID HEAR ABOUT THE BARD THAT THE PREFECT OF GAUL GAVE CAESAR AS A PRESENT...
IT SEEMS THAT THIS BARD IS TO BE THROWN TO THE LIONS AT THE NEXT GAMES IN THE CIRCUS MAXIMUS, IN A FEW DAYS' TIME...
!!
WE'LL RESCUE HIM!
YOU CAN'T. THE BARD'S BEEN SHUT UP IN A CELL IN THE CIRCUS... AND IT'S A MAXIMUM SECURITY CIRCUS!
BUT THERE'S WORSE TO COME. THAT'S WHY I WARNED YOU TO BE CAREFUL. YOU MUST BE INDOMITABLE GAULS LIKE THE BARD! YOU MUST FLEE FROM ROME!
CAIUS FATUOUS, WHO TRAINS THE GLADIATORS, IS LOOKING FOR MEN FOR THE GAMES... AND INDOMITABLE GAULS ARE IN GREAT DEMAND!
WE WILL RESCUE OUR BARD!
YOU ACT THE FINE LADY AND YOU CAN'T EVEN AFFORD A SLAVE TO DO THE HOUSEWORK!
SO I AM A FINE LADY! SO YOU KNOW WHAT THE FINE LADY HAS TO SAY TO YOU?
BY JUNO, IF YOU DON'T SHUT UP I'M CALLING THE WATCH!
THESE ROMANS ARE CRAZY!
THERE THEY ARE!
WE'RE BEING ATTACKED!
GOODY!
LOOK, ASTERIX! I'VE THOUGHT OF SOMETHING NEW! LOOK, I DON'T EVEN TOUCH THEM, I SHAKE THEM! IT LASTS LONGER THAT WAY!
ALL RIGHT, OBELIX. PUT HIM DOWN NOW!
WILL YOU BE QUIET OUT THERE IN THE ROAD! WE CAN'T HEAR OURSELVES SHOUT IN HERE!
19

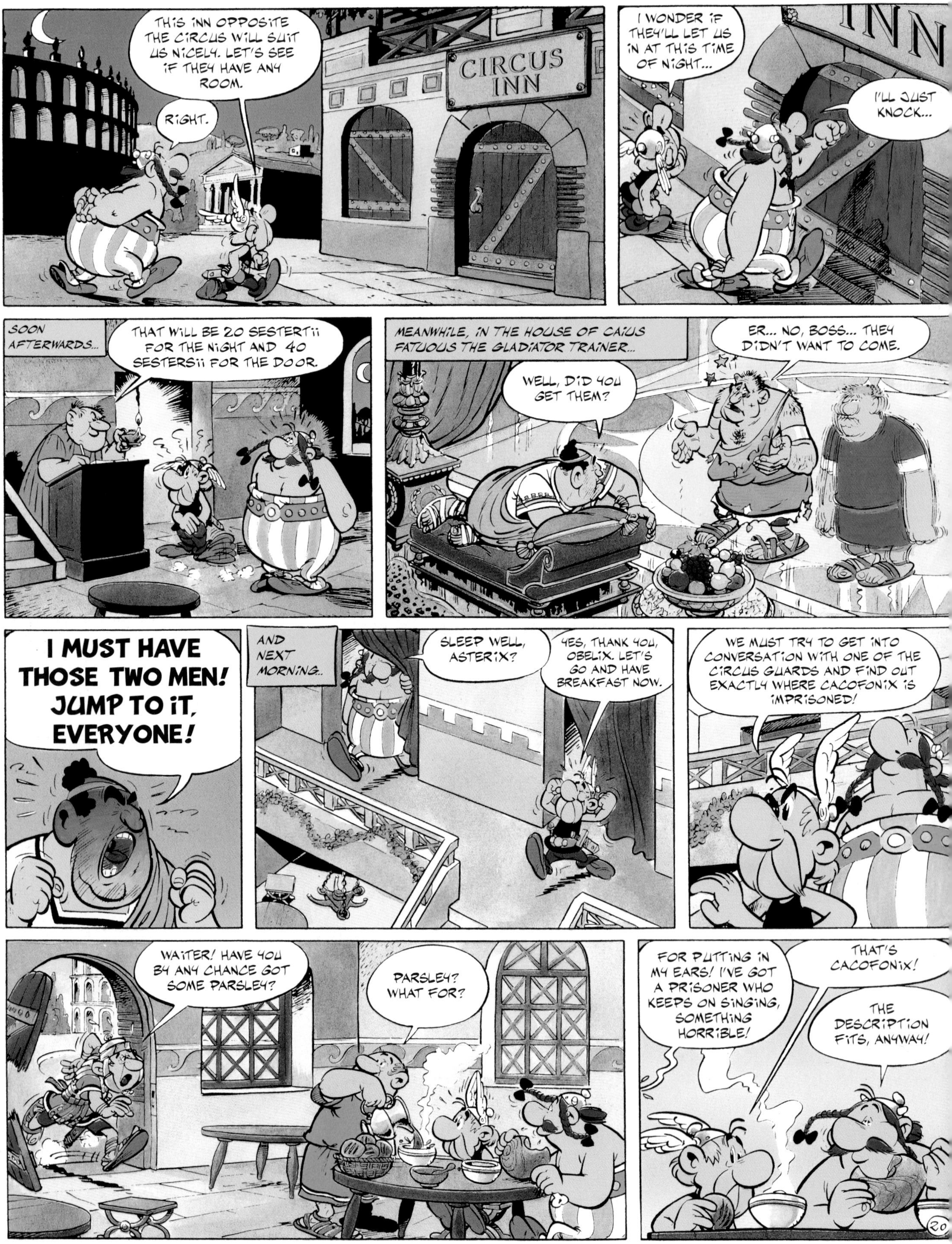
THIS INN OPPOSITE THE CIRCUS WILL SUIT US NICELY. LET'S SEE IF THEY HAVE ANY ROOM.
RIGHT.
CIRCUS INN
I WONDER IF THEY'LL LET US IN AT THIS TIME OF NIGHT...
INN
I'LL JUST KNOCK...
SOON AFTERWARDS...
THAT WILL BE 20 SESTERTII FOR THE NIGHT AND 40 SESTERSII FOR THE DOOR.
MEANWHILE, IN THE HOUSE OF CAIUS FATUOUS THE GLADIATOR TRAINER...
WELL, DID YOU GET THEM?
ER... NO, BOSS... THEY DIDN'T WANT TO COME.
I MUST HAVE THOSE TWO MEN! JUMP TO IT, EVERYONE!
AND NEXT MORNING...
SLEEP WELL, ASTERIX?
YES, THANK YOU, OBELIX. LET'S GO AND HAVE BREAKFAST NOW.
WE MUST TRY TO GET INTO CONVERSATION WITH ONE OF THE CIRCUS GUARDS AND FIND OUT EXACTLY WHERE CACOFONIX IS IMPRISONED!
WAITER! HAVE YOU BY ANY CHANCE GOT SOME PARSLEY?
PARSLEY? WHAT FOR?
FOR PUTTING IN MY EARS! I'VE GOT A PRISONER WHO KEEPS ON SINGING, SOMETHING HORRIBLE!
THAT'S CACOFONIX!
THE DESCRIPTION FITS, ANYWAY!
20

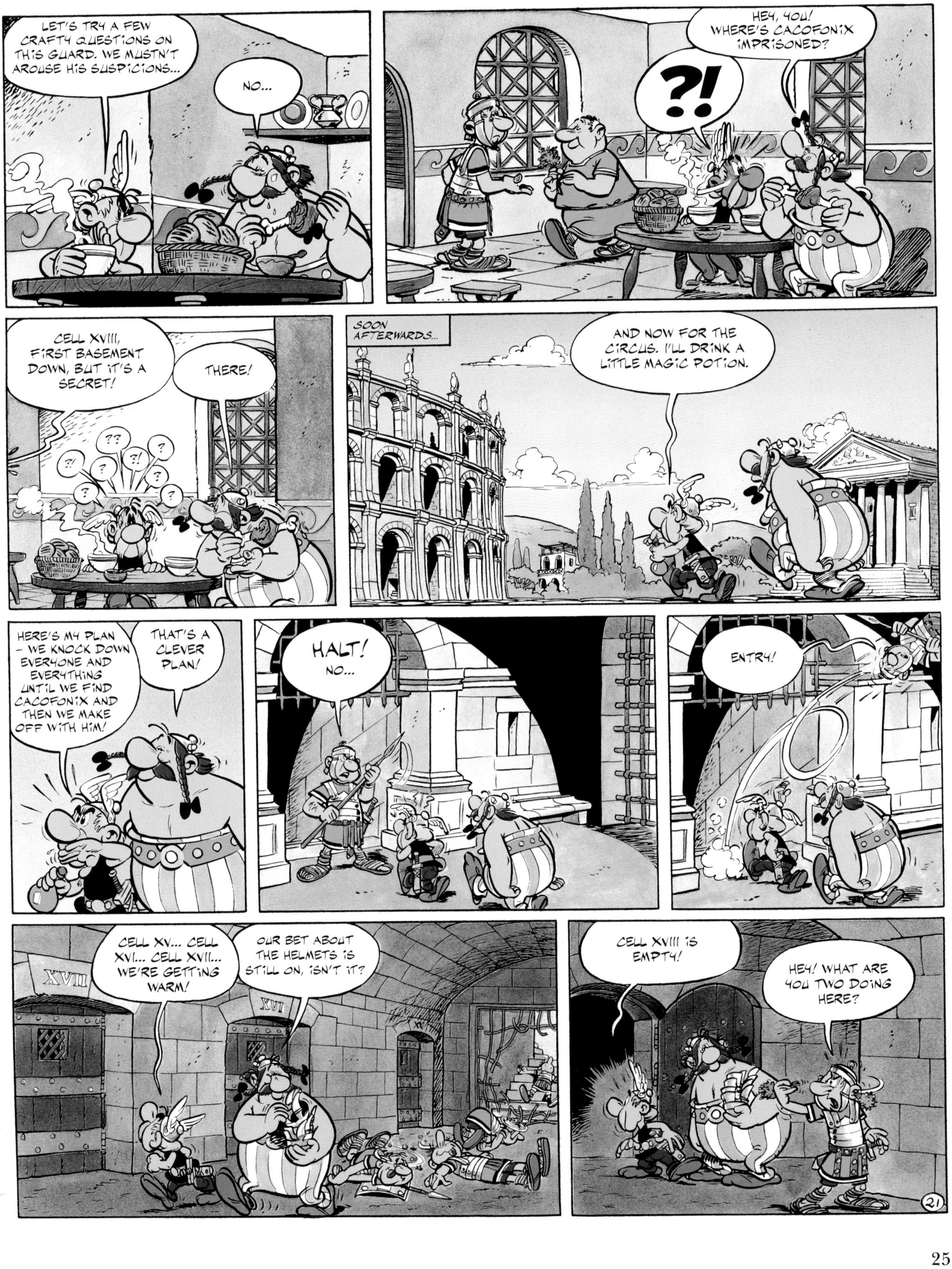
LET'S TRY A FEW CRAFTY QUESTIONS ON THIS GUARD. WE MUSTN'T AROUSE HIS SUSPICIONS...
NO...
HEY, YOU! WHERE'S CACOFONIX IMPRISONED?
?!
CELL XVIII, FIRST BASEMENT DOWN, BUT IT'S A SECRET!
THERE!
SOON AFTERWARDS...
AND NOW FOR THE CIRCUS. I'LL DRINK A LITTLE MAGIC POTION.
HERE'S MY PLAN – WE KNOCK DOWN EVERYONE AND EVERYTHING UNTIL WE FIND CACOFONIX AND THEN WE MAKE OFF WITH HIM!
THAT'S A CLEVER PLAN!
HALT! NO...
ENTRY!
CELL XV... CELL XVI... CELL XVII... WE'RE GETTING WARM!
OUR BET ABOUT THE HELMETS IS STILL ON, ISN'T IT?
XVII
XVI
CELL XVIII IS EMPTY!
HEY! WHAT ARE YOU TWO DOING HERE?
21

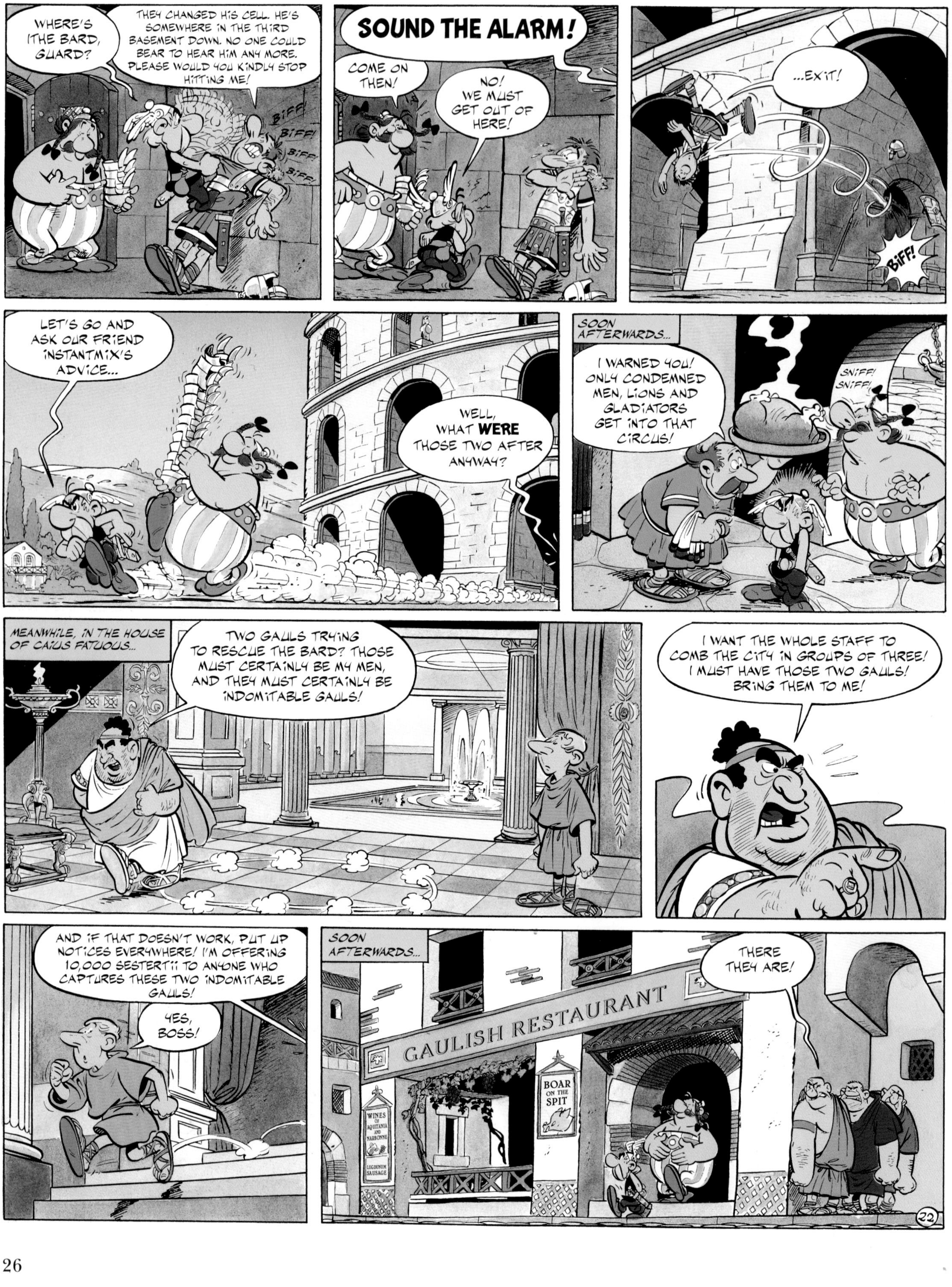

WHERE'S THE BARD, GUARD?
THEY CHANGED HIS CELL. HE'S SOMEWHERE IN THE THIRD BASEMENT DOWN. NO ONE COULD BEAR TO HEAR HIM ANY MORE. PLEASE WOULD YOU KINDLY STOP HITTING ME!
BIFF! BIFF! BIFF! BIFF!
SOUND THE ALARM!
COME ON THEN!
NO! WE MUST GET OUT OF HERE!
...EXIT!
BIFF!
LET'S GO AND ASK OUR FRIEND INSTANTMIX'S ADVICE...
WELL, WHAT WERE THOSE TWO AFTER ANYWAY?
SOON AFTERWARDS...
I WARNED YOU! ONLY CONDEMNED MEN, LIONS AND GLADIATORS GET INTO THAT CIRCUS!
SNIFF! SNIFF!
MEANWHILE, IN THE HOUSE OF CAIUS FATUOUS...
TWO GAULS TRYING TO RESCUE THE BARD? THOSE MUST CERTAINLY BE MY MEN, AND THEY MUST CERTAINLY BE INDOMITABLE GAULS!
I WANT THE WHOLE STAFF TO COMB THE CITY IN GROUPS OF THREE! I MUST HAVE THOSE TWO GAULS! BRING THEM TO ME!
AND IF THAT DOESN'T WORK, PUT UP NOTICES EVERYWHERE! I'M OFFERING 10,000 SESTERTII TO ANYONE WHO CAPTURES THESE TWO INDOMITABLE GAULS!
YES, BOSS!
SOON AFTERWARDS...
GAULISH RESTAURANT
BOAR ON THE SPIT
WINES OF AQUITANIA AND NARBONNE
LUGDUNUM SAUSAGE
THERE THEY ARE!
22

LET'S GET THEM!

SPLAT!

IT'S A NUISANCE, WHAT INSTANTMIX TOLD US...

CLONK!

YES, HEARING THINGS LIKE THAT MAKES ME COME OVER ALL FAINT...

HE SAID ONLY CONDEMNED MEN, LIONS AND GLADIATORS GET INTO THE CIRCUS...

SUPPOSE WE DRESSED UP AS LIONS?

GAULISH RESTAURANT

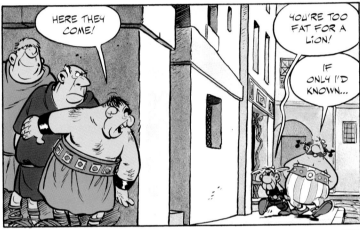

HERE THEY COME!

YOU'RE TOO FAT FOR A LION!

IF ONLY I'D KNOWN...

ALL THE SAME, WE MUST SAVE OUR BARD!

OF COURSE!

LET'S BEAT IT! HERE COME THE COPS!

NOW, NOW, NOW, WHAT'S ALL THIS 'ERE? YOU COME ALONG QUIETLY TO THE STATION! AND NO FUNNY BUSINESS – WE'RE SEVEN TO TWO!

LET'S GET BACK TO OUR INN!

FORWARD, MEN... OUFF!

I SAY, ASTERIX, DON'T YOU THINK IT'S FUNNY, ALL THESE PEOPLE ATTACKING US?

PEOPLE? WHAT PEOPLE?

CIRCUS INN

23

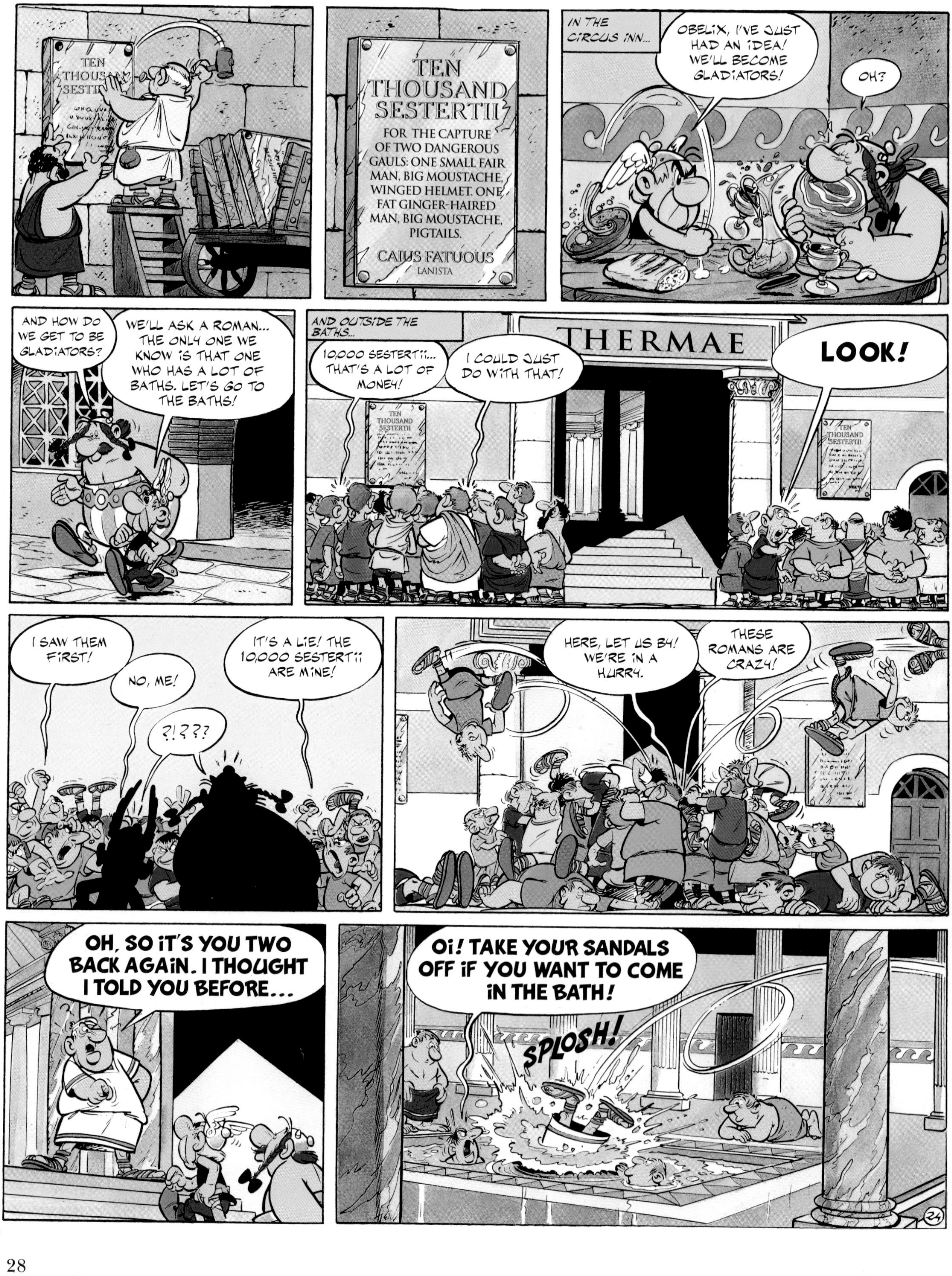

TEN THOUSAND SESTERTII
FOR THE CAPTURE OF TWO DANGEROUS GAULS: ONE SMALL FAIR MAN, BIG MOUSTACHE, WINGED HELMET. ONE FAT GINGER-HAIRED MAN, BIG MOUSTACHE, PIGTAILS.
CAIUS FATUOUS
LANISTA
IN THE CIRCUS INN...
OBELIX, I'VE JUST HAD AN IDEA! WE'LL BECOME GLADIATORS!
OH?
AND HOW DO WE GET TO BE GLADIATORS?
WE'LL ASK A ROMAN... THE ONLY ONE WE KNOW IS THAT ONE WHO HAS A LOT OF BATHS. LET'S GO TO THE BATHS!
AND OUTSIDE THE BATHS...
THERMAE
10,000 SESTERTII... THAT'S A LOT OF MONEY!
I COULD JUST DO WITH THAT!
LOOK!
I SAW THEM FIRST!
NO, ME!
?!???
IT'S A LIE! THE 10,000 SESTERTII ARE MINE!
HERE, LET US BY! WE'RE IN A HURRY.
THESE ROMANS ARE CRAZY!
OH, SO IT'S YOU TWO BACK AGAIN. I THOUGHT I TOLD YOU BEFORE...
OI! TAKE YOUR SANDALS OFF IF YOU WANT TO COME IN THE BATH!
SPLOSH!
24

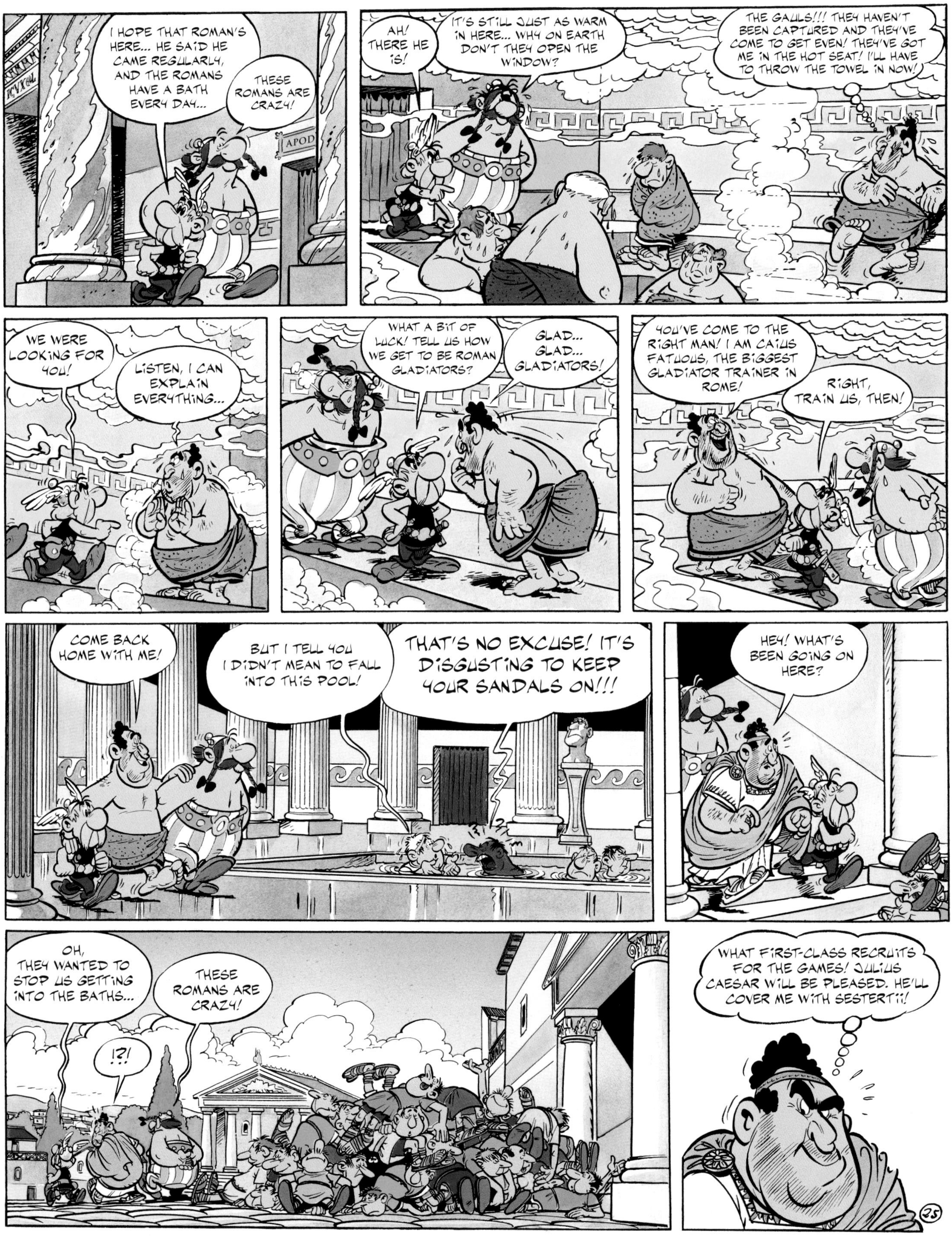
I HOPE THAT ROMAN'S HERE... HE SAID HE CAME REGULARLY, AND THE ROMANS HAVE A BATH EVERY DAY...
THESE ROMANS ARE CRAZY!
APOD
AH! THERE HE IS!
IT'S STILL JUST AS WARM IN HERE... WHY ON EARTH DON'T THEY OPEN THE WINDOW?
THE GAULS!!! THEY HAVEN'T BEEN CAPTURED AND THEY'VE COME TO GET EVEN! THEY'VE GOT ME IN THE HOT SEAT! I'LL HAVE TO THROW THE TOWEL IN NOW!
WE WERE LOOKING FOR YOU!
LISTEN, I CAN EXPLAIN EVERYTHING...
WHAT A BIT OF LUCK! TELL US HOW WE GET TO BE ROMAN GLADIATORS?
GLAD... GLAD... GLADIATORS!
YOU'VE COME TO THE RIGHT MAN! I AM CAIUS FATUOUS, THE BIGGEST GLADIATOR TRAINER IN ROME!
RIGHT, TRAIN US, THEN!
COME BACK HOME WITH ME!
BUT I TELL YOU I DIDN'T MEAN TO FALL INTO THIS POOL!
THAT'S NO EXCUSE! IT'S DISGUSTING TO KEEP YOUR SANDALS ON!!!
HEY! WHAT'S BEEN GOING ON HERE?
OH, THEY WANTED TO STOP US GETTING INTO THE BATHS...
THESE ROMANS ARE CRAZY!
!?!
WHAT FIRST-CLASS RECRUITS FOR THE GAMES! JULIUS CAESAR WILL BE PLEASED. HE'LL COVER ME WITH SESTERTII!
25

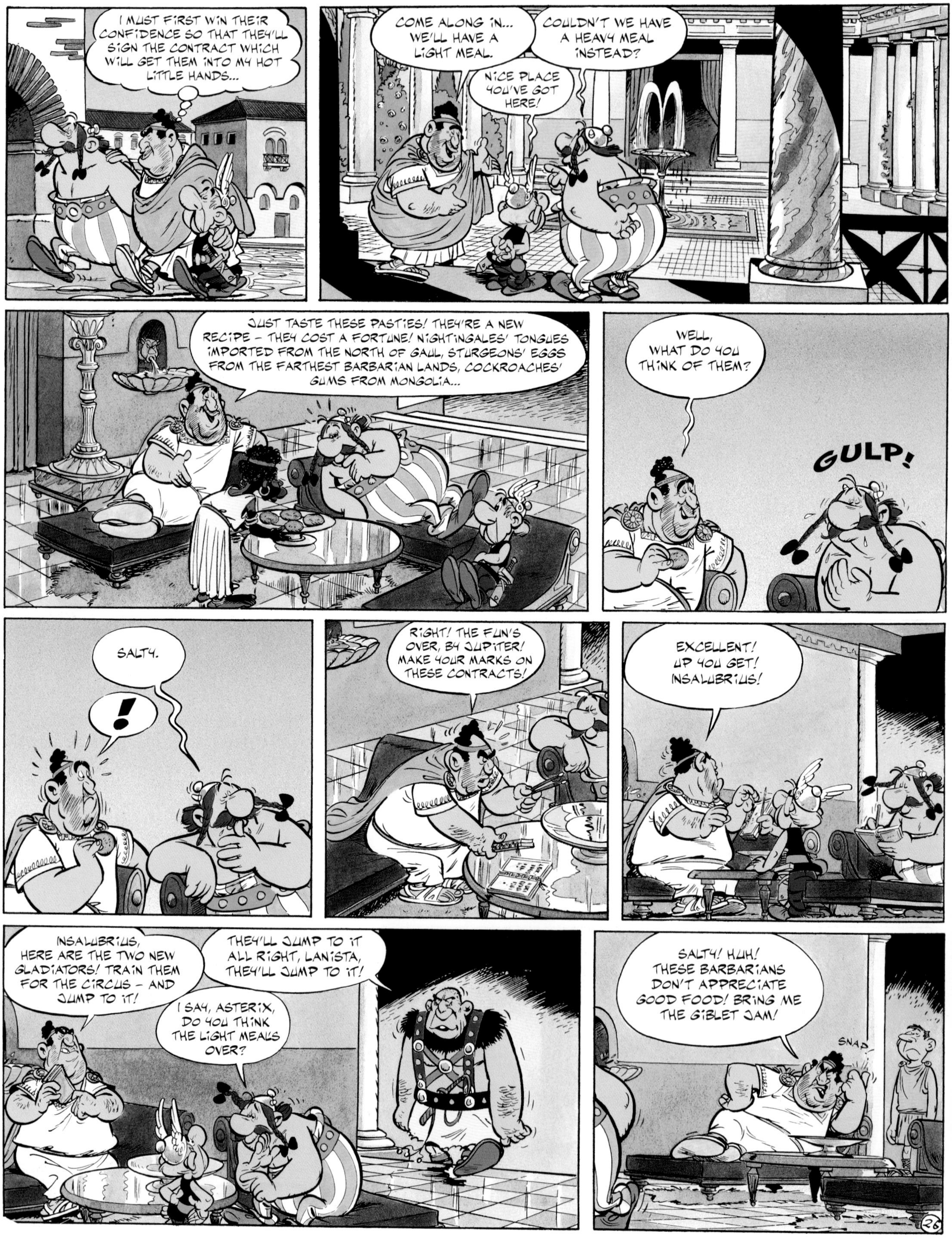
I MUST FIRST WIN THEIR CONFIDENCE SO THAT THEY'LL SIGN THE CONTRACT WHICH WILL GET THEM INTO MY HOT LITTLE HANDS...
COME ALONG IN... WE'LL HAVE A LIGHT MEAL.
COULDN'T WE HAVE A HEAVY MEAL INSTEAD?
NICE PLACE YOU'VE GOT HERE!
JUST TASTE THESE PASTIES! THEY'RE A NEW RECIPE – THEY COST A FORTUNE! NIGHTINGALES' TONGUES IMPORTED FROM THE NORTH OF GAUL, STURGEONS' EGGS FROM THE FARTHEST BARBARIAN LANDS, COCKROACHES' GUMS FROM MONGOLIA...
WELL, WHAT DO YOU THINK OF THEM?
GULP!
SALTY.
!
RIGHT! THE FUN'S OVER, BY JUPITER! MAKE YOUR MARKS ON THESE CONTRACTS!
EXCELLENT! UP YOU GET! INSALUBRIUS!
INSALUBRIUS, HERE ARE THE TWO NEW GLADIATORS! TRAIN THEM FOR THE CIRCUS – AND JUMP TO IT!
THEY'LL JUMP TO IT ALL RIGHT, LANISTA, THEY'LL JUMP TO IT!
I SAY, ASTERIX, DO YOU THINK THE LIGHT MEAL'S OVER?
SALTY! HUH! THESE BARBARIANS DON'T APPRECIATE GOOD FOOD! BRING ME THE GIBLET JAM!
SNAP
26

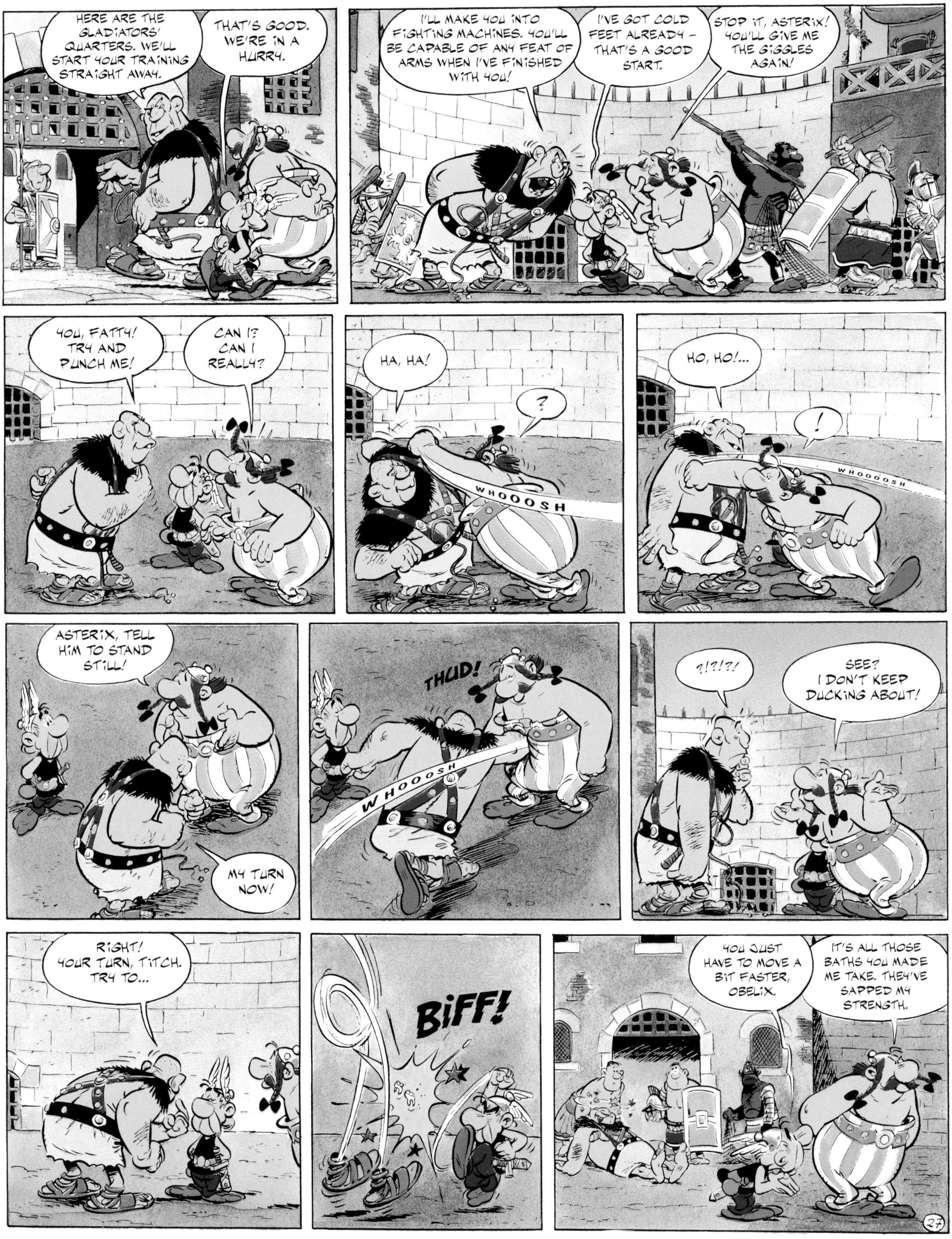
HERE ARE THE GLADIATORS' QUARTERS. WE'LL START YOUR TRAINING STRAIGHT AWAY.
THAT'S GOOD. WE'RE IN A HURRY.
I'LL MAKE YOU INTO FIGHTING MACHINES. YOU'LL BE CAPABLE OF ANY FEAT OF ARMS WHEN I'VE FINISHED WITH YOU!
I'VE GOT COLD FEET ALREADY – THAT'S A GOOD START.
STOP IT, ASTERIX! YOU'LL GIVE ME THE GIGGLES AGAIN!
YOU, FATTY! TRY AND PUNCH ME!
CAN I? CAN I REALLY?
HA, HA!
WHOOOSH
?
HO, HO!...
!
WHOOOOSH
ASTERIX, TELL HIM TO STAND STILL!
MY TURN NOW!
THUD!
WHOOOSH
?!?!?!
SEE? I DON'T KEEP DUCKING ABOUT!
RIGHT! YOUR TURN, TITCH. TRY TO...
BIFF!
YOU JUST HAVE TO MOVE A BIT FASTER, OBELIX.
IT'S ALL THOSE BATHS YOU MADE ME TAKE. THEY'VE SAPPED MY STRENGTH.
27

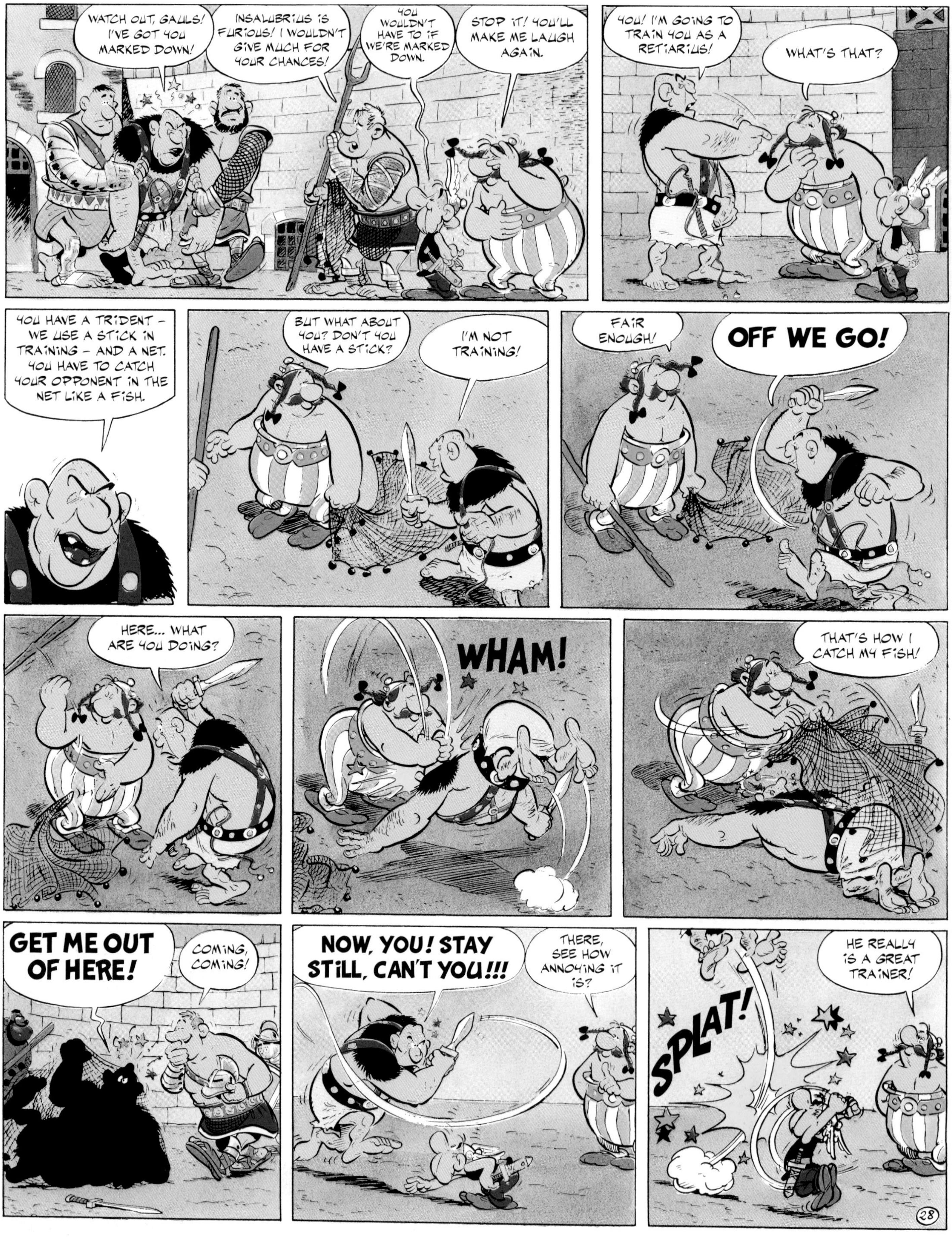
WATCH OUT, GAULS! I'VE GOT YOU MARKED DOWN!
INSALUBRIUS IS FURIOUS! I WOULDN'T GIVE MUCH FOR YOUR CHANCES!
YOU WOULDN'T HAVE TO IF WE'RE MARKED DOWN.
STOP IT! YOU'LL MAKE ME LAUGH AGAIN.
YOU! I'M GOING TO TRAIN YOU AS A RETIARIUS!
WHAT'S THAT?
YOU HAVE A TRIDENT – WE USE A STICK IN TRAINING – AND A NET. YOU HAVE TO CATCH YOUR OPPONENT IN THE NET LIKE A FISH.
BUT WHAT ABOUT YOU? DON'T YOU HAVE A STICK?
I'M NOT TRAINING!
FAIR ENOUGH!
OFF WE GO!
HERE... WHAT ARE YOU DOING?
WHAM!
THAT'S HOW I CATCH MY FISH!
GET ME OUT OF HERE!
COMING, COMING!
NOW, YOU! STAY STILL, CAN'T YOU!!!
THERE, SEE HOW ANNOYING IT IS?
SPLAT!
HE REALLY IS A GREAT TRAINER!
28

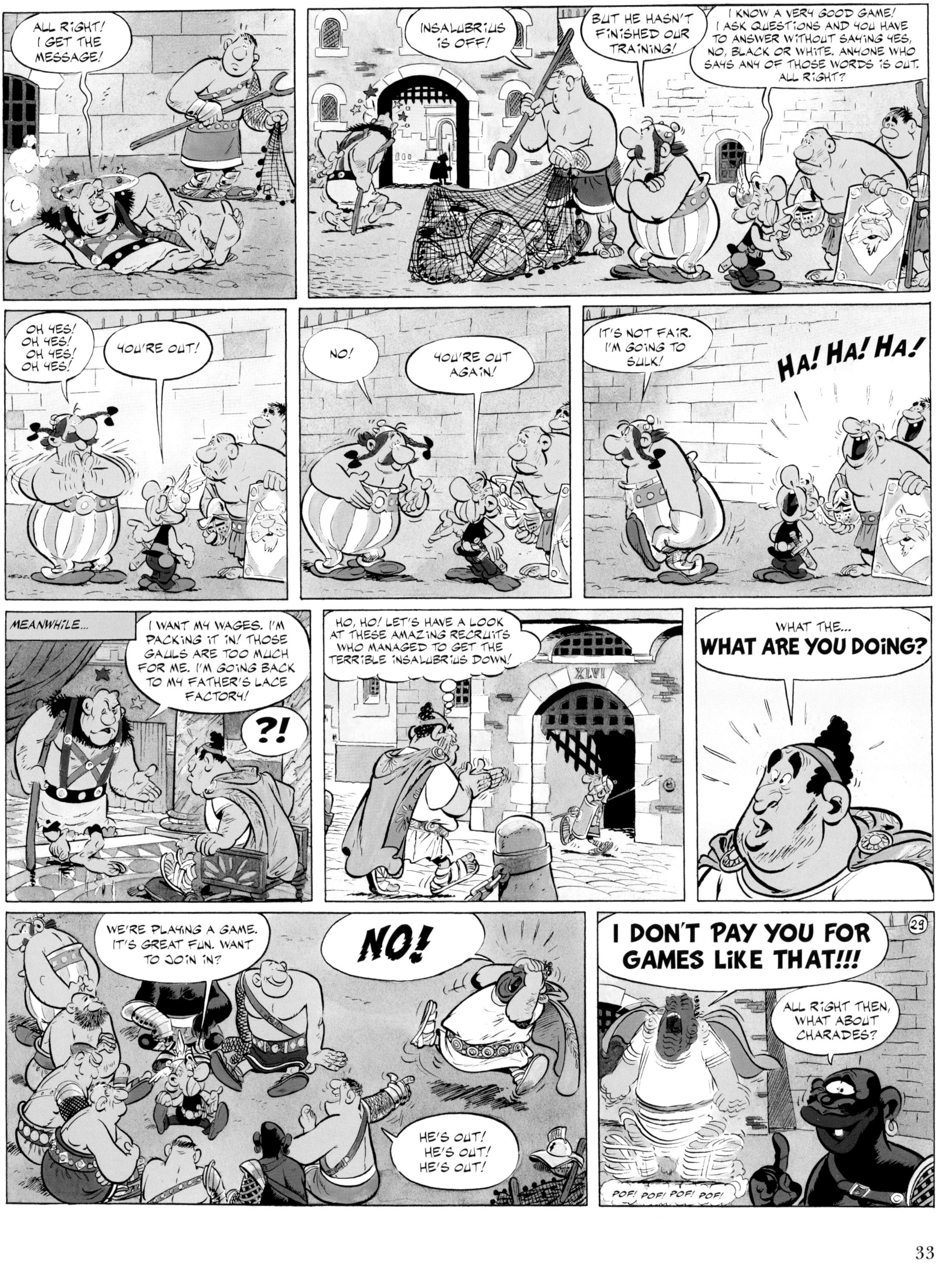

ALL RIGHT! I GET THE MESSAGE!
INSALUBRIUS IS OFF!
BUT HE HASN'T FINISHED OUR TRAINING!
I KNOW A VERY GOOD GAME! I ASK QUESTIONS AND YOU HAVE TO ANSWER WITHOUT SAYING YES, NO, BLACK OR WHITE. ANYONE WHO SAYS ANY OF THOSE WORDS IS OUT. ALL RIGHT?
OH YES! OH YES! OH YES! OH YES!
YOU'RE OUT!
NO!
YOU'RE OUT AGAIN!
IT'S NOT FAIR. I'M GOING TO SULK!
HA! HA! HA!
MEANWHILE...
I WANT MY WAGES. I'M PACKING IT IN! THOSE GAULS ARE TOO MUCH FOR ME. I'M GOING BACK TO MY FATHER'S LACE FACTORY!
?!
HO, HO! LET'S HAVE A LOOK AT THESE AMAZING RECRUITS WHO MANAGED TO GET THE TERRIBLE INSALUBRIUS DOWN!
XLVI
WHAT THE...
WHAT ARE YOU DOING?
WE'RE PLAYING A GAME. IT'S GREAT FUN. WANT TO JOIN IN?
NO!
HE'S OUT! HE'S OUT! HE'S OUT!
I DON'T PAY YOU FOR GAMES LIKE THAT!!!
29
ALL RIGHT THEN, WHAT ABOUT CHARADES?
POF! POF! POF! POF!

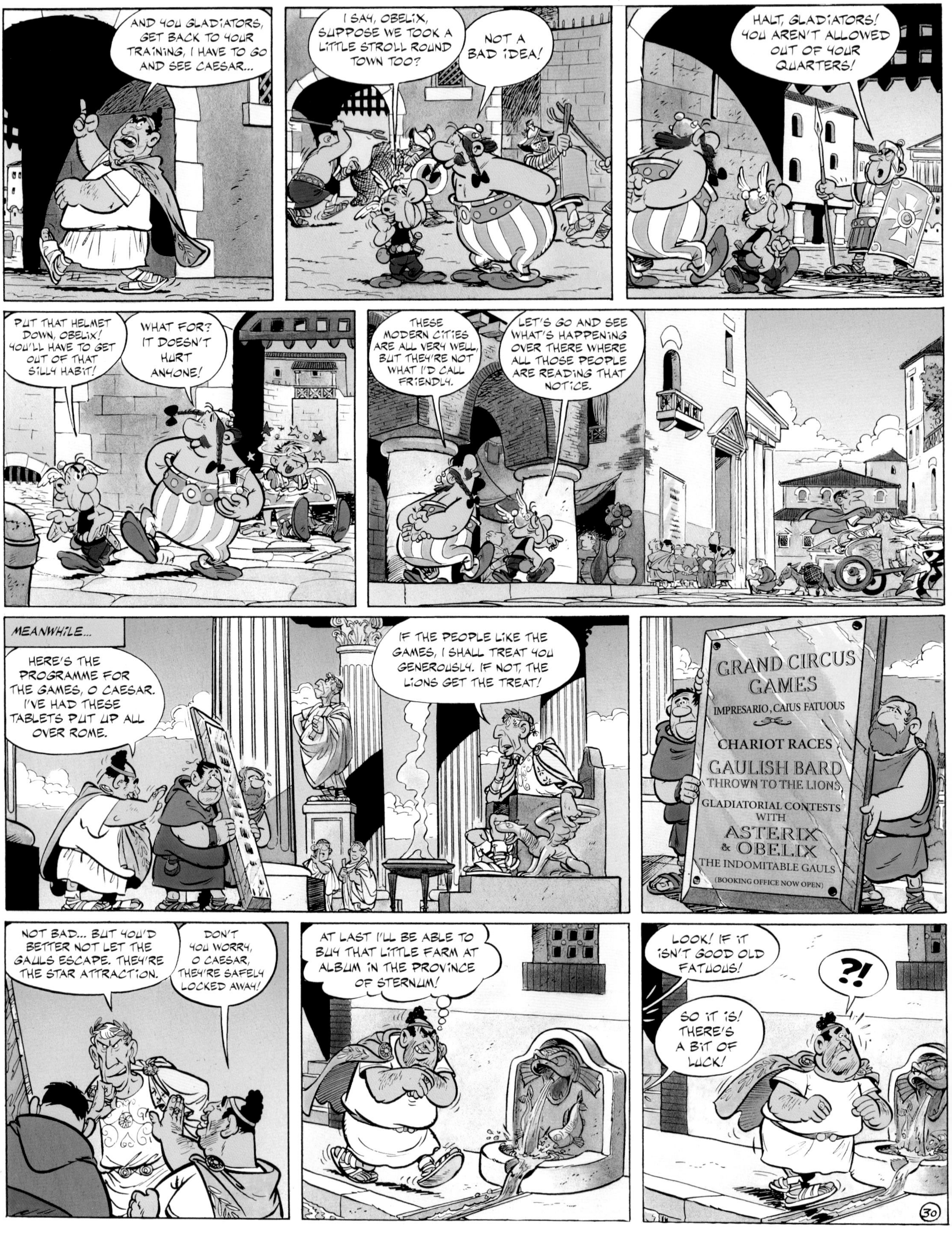
AND YOU GLADIATORS, GET BACK TO YOUR TRAINING, I HAVE TO GO AND SEE CAESAR...
I SAY, OBELIX, SUPPOSE WE TOOK A LITTLE STROLL ROUND TOWN TOO?
NOT A BAD IDEA!
HALT, GLADIATORS! YOU AREN'T ALLOWED OUT OF YOUR QUARTERS!
PUT THAT HELMET DOWN, OBELIX! YOU'LL HAVE TO GET OUT OF THAT SILLY HABIT!
WHAT FOR? IT DOESN'T HURT ANYONE!
THESE MODERN CITIES ARE ALL VERY WELL, BUT THEY'RE NOT WHAT I'D CALL FRIENDLY.
LET'S GO AND SEE WHAT'S HAPPENING OVER THERE WHERE ALL THOSE PEOPLE ARE READING THAT NOTICE.
MEANWHILE...
HERE'S THE PROGRAMME FOR THE GAMES, O CAESAR. I'VE HAD THESE TABLETS PUT UP ALL OVER ROME.
IF THE PEOPLE LIKE THE GAMES, I SHALL TREAT YOU GENEROUSLY. IF NOT, THE LIONS GET THE TREAT!
GRAND CIRCUS GAMES
IMPRESARIO, CAIUS FATUOUS
CHARIOT RACES
GAULISH BARD THROWN TO THE LIONS
GLADIATORIAL CONTESTS WITH
ASTERIX & OBELIX
THE INDOMITABLE GAULS
(BOOKING OFFICE NOW OPEN)
NOT BAD... BUT YOU'D BETTER NOT LET THE GAULS ESCAPE. THEY'RE THE STAR ATTRACTION.
DON'T YOU WORRY, O CAESAR, THEY'RE SAFELY LOCKED AWAY!
AT LAST I'LL BE ABLE TO BUY THAT LITTLE FARM AT ALBUM IN THE PROVINCE OF STERNUM!
LOOK! IF IT ISN'T GOOD OLD FATUOUS!
?!
SO IT IS! THERE'S A BIT OF LUCK!
30

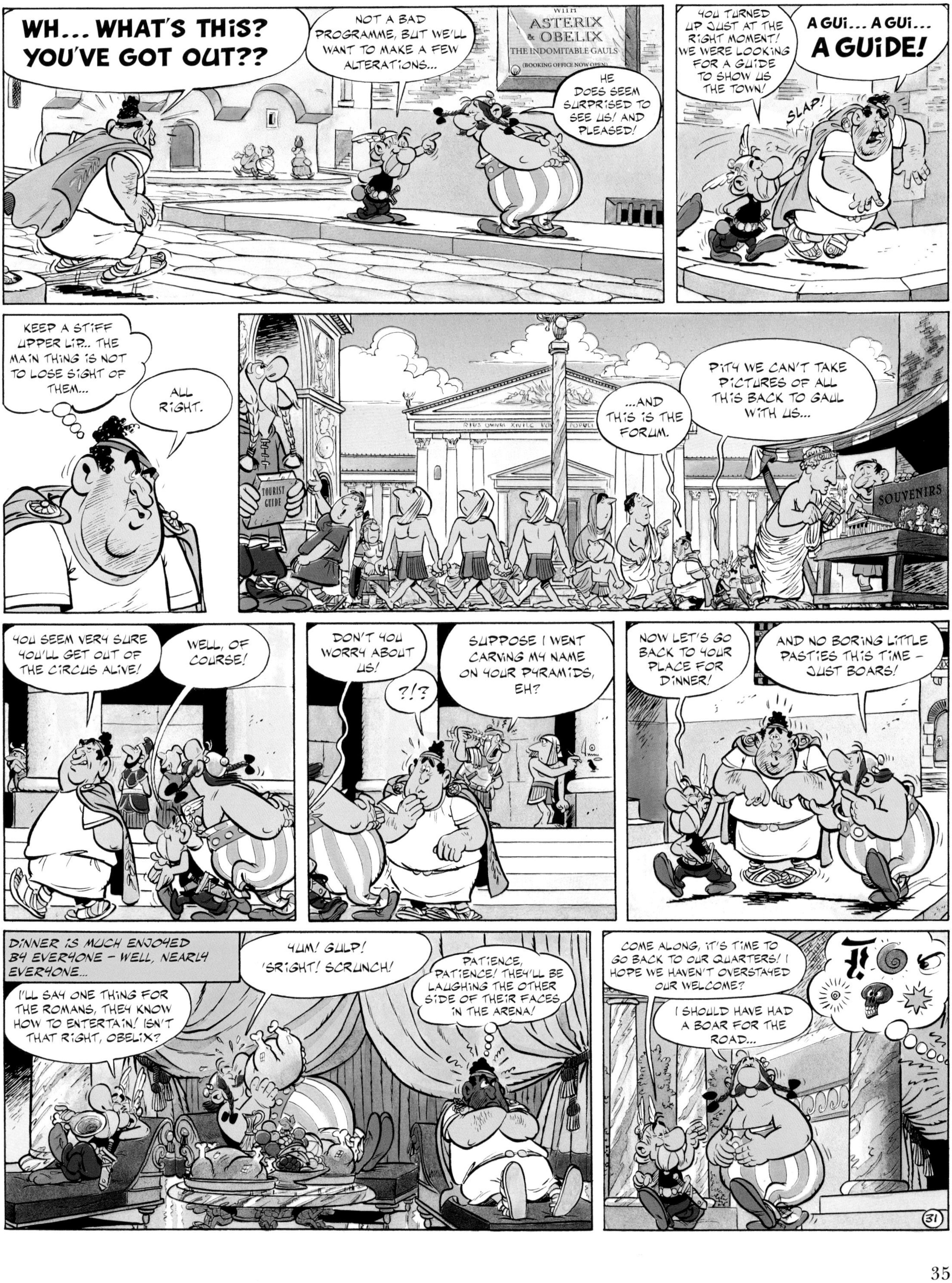
WH... WHAT'S THIS? YOU'VE GOT OUT??
NOT A BAD PROGRAMME, BUT WE'LL WANT TO MAKE A FEW ALTERATIONS...
WITH ASTERIX & OBELIX THE INDOMITABLE GAULS (BOOKING OFFICE NOW OPEN)
HE DOES SEEM SURPRISED TO SEE US! AND PLEASED!
YOU TURNED UP JUST AT THE RIGHT MOMENT! WE WERE LOOKING FOR A GUIDE TO SHOW US THE TOWN!
A GUI... A GUI... A GUIDE!
SLAP!
KEEP A STIFF UPPER LIP.. THE MAIN THING IS NOT TO LOSE SIGHT OF THEM...
ALL RIGHT.
TOURIST GUIDE
...AND THIS IS THE FORUM.
PITY WE CAN'T TAKE PICTURES OF ALL THIS BACK TO GAUL WITH US...
SOUVENIRS
YOU SEEM VERY SURE YOU'LL GET OUT OF THE CIRCUS ALIVE!
WELL, OF COURSE!
DON'T YOU WORRY ABOUT US!
?!?
SUPPOSE I WENT CARVING MY NAME ON YOUR PYRAMIDS, EH?
NOW LET'S GO BACK TO YOUR PLACE FOR DINNER!
AND NO BORING LITTLE PASTIES THIS TIME - JUST BOARS!
DINNER IS MUCH ENJOYED BY EVERYONE - WELL, NEARLY EVERYONE...
I'LL SAY ONE THING FOR THE ROMANS, THEY KNOW HOW TO ENTERTAIN! ISN'T THAT RIGHT, OBELIX?
YUM! GULP! 'SRIGHT! SCRUNCH!
PATIENCE, PATIENCE! THEY'LL BE LAUGHING THE OTHER SIDE OF THEIR FACES IN THE ARENA!
COME ALONG, IT'S TIME TO GO BACK TO OUR QUARTERS! I HOPE WE HAVEN'T OVERSTAYED OUR WELCOME?
I SHOULD HAVE HAD A BOAR FOR THE ROAD...
31

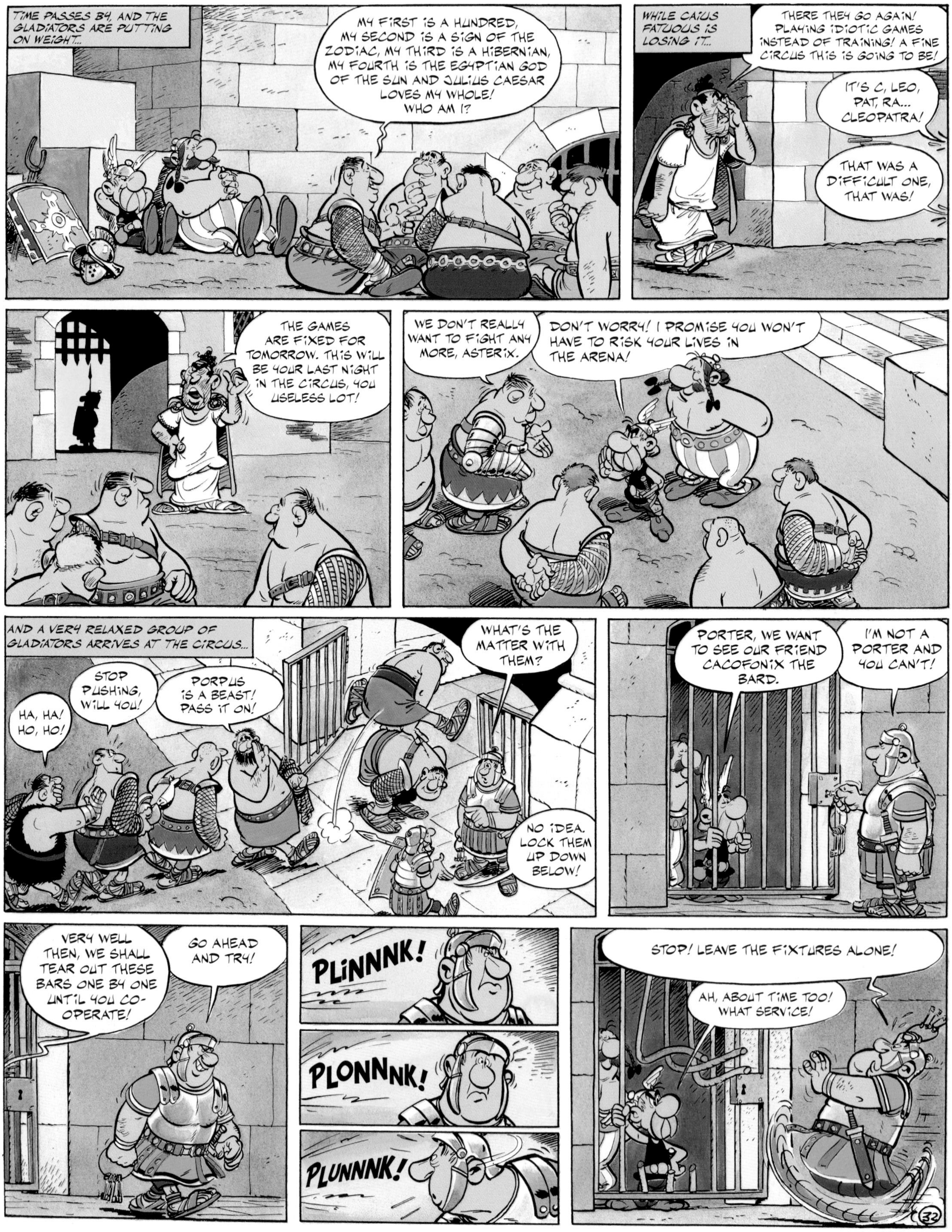
TIME PASSES BY, AND THE GLADIATORS ARE PUTTING ON WEIGHT...
MY FIRST IS A HUNDRED, MY SECOND IS A SIGN OF THE ZODIAC, MY THIRD IS A HIBERNIAN, MY FOURTH IS THE EGYPTIAN GOD OF THE SUN AND JULIUS CAESAR LOVES MY WHOLE! WHO AM I?
WHILE CAIUS FATUOUS IS LOSING IT...
THERE THEY GO AGAIN! PLAYING IDIOTIC GAMES INSTEAD OF TRAINING! A FINE CIRCUS THIS IS GOING TO BE!
IT'S C, LEO, PAT, RA... CLEOPATRA!
THAT WAS A DIFFICULT ONE, THAT WAS!
THE GAMES ARE FIXED FOR TOMORROW. THIS WILL BE YOUR LAST NIGHT IN THE CIRCUS, YOU USELESS LOT!
WE DON'T REALLY WANT TO FIGHT ANY MORE, ASTERIX.
DON'T WORRY! I PROMISE YOU WON'T HAVE TO RISK YOUR LIVES IN THE ARENA!
AND A VERY RELAXED GROUP OF GLADIATORS ARRIVES AT THE CIRCUS...
HA, HA! HO, HO!
STOP PUSHING, WILL YOU!
PORPUS IS A BEAST! PASS IT ON!
WHAT'S THE MATTER WITH THEM?
NO IDEA. LOCK THEM UP DOWN BELOW!
PORTER, WE WANT TO SEE OUR FRIEND CACOFONIX THE BARD.
I'M NOT A PORTER AND YOU CAN'T!
VERY WELL THEN, WE SHALL TEAR OUT THESE BARS ONE BY ONE UNTIL YOU CO-OPERATE!
GO AHEAD AND TRY!
PLINNNK!
PLONNNNK!
PLUNNNK!
STOP! LEAVE THE FIXTURES ALONE!
AH, ABOUT TIME TOO! WHAT SERVICE!
32

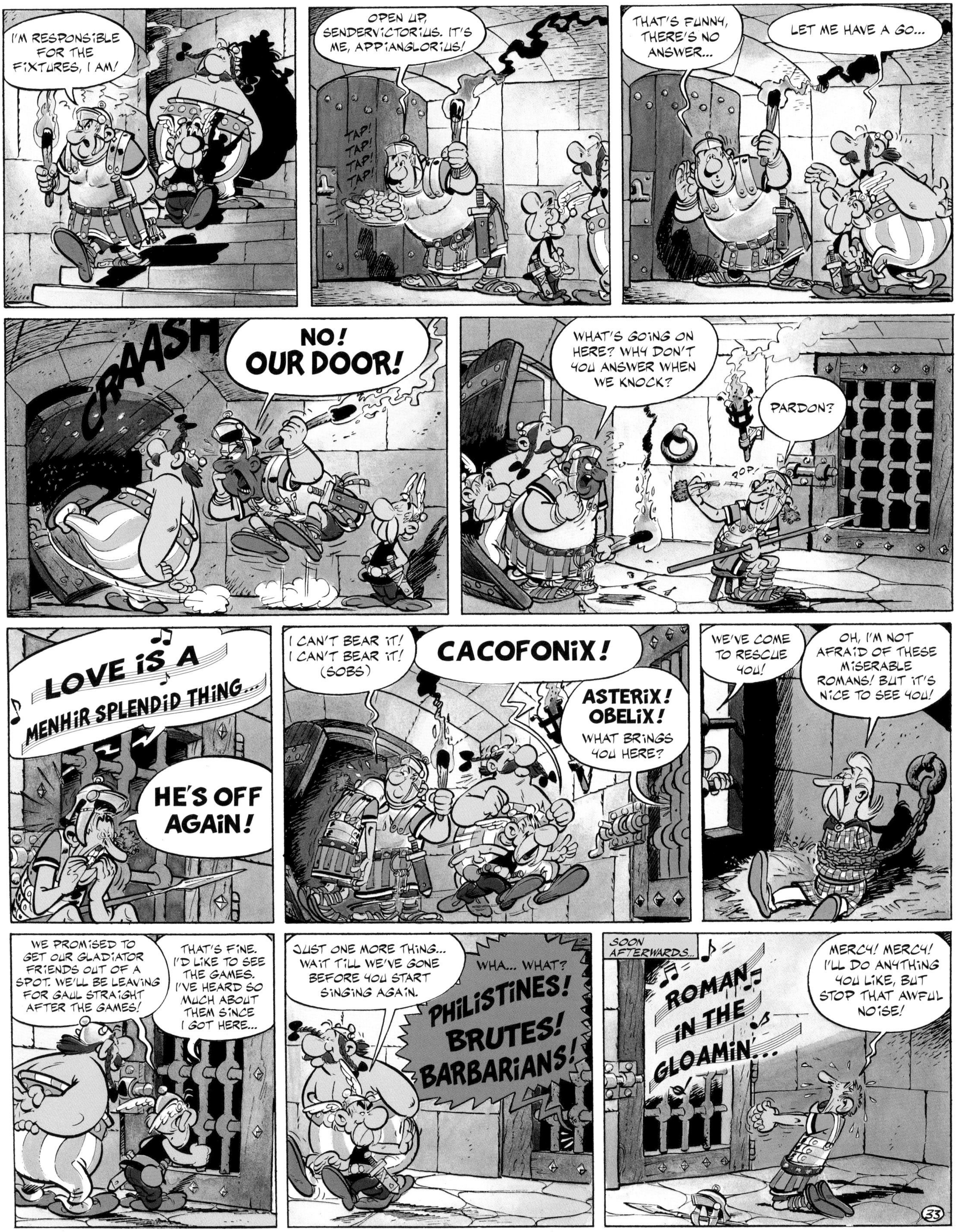

I'M RESPONSIBLE FOR THE FIXTURES, I AM!
OPEN UP, SENDERVICTORIUS. IT'S ME, APPIANGLORIUS!
TAP! TAP! TAP! TAP!
THAT'S FUNNY, THERE'S NO ANSWER...
LET ME HAVE A GO...
CRAASH
NO! OUR DOOR!
WHAT'S GOING ON HERE? WHY DON'T YOU ANSWER WHEN WE KNOCK?
PARDON?
POP!
LOVE IS A MENHIR SPLENDID THING...
HE'S OFF AGAIN!
I CAN'T BEAR IT! I CAN'T BEAR IT! (SOBS)
CACOFONIX!
ASTERIX! OBELIX! WHAT BRINGS YOU HERE?
WE'VE COME TO RESCUE YOU!
OH, I'M NOT AFRAID OF THESE MISERABLE ROMANS! BUT IT'S NICE TO SEE YOU!
WE PROMISED TO GET OUR GLADIATOR FRIENDS OUT OF A SPOT. WE'LL BE LEAVING FOR GAUL STRAIGHT AFTER THE GAMES!
THAT'S FINE. I'D LIKE TO SEE THE GAMES. I'VE HEARD SO MUCH ABOUT THEM SINCE I GOT HERE...
JUST ONE MORE THING... WAIT TILL WE'VE GONE BEFORE YOU START SINGING AGAIN.
WHA... WHAT?
PHILISTINES! BRUTES! BARBARIANS!
SOON AFTERWARDS...
ROMAN IN THE GLOAMIN'...
MERCY! MERCY! I'LL DO ANYTHING YOU LIKE, BUT STOP THAT AWFUL NOISE!
33

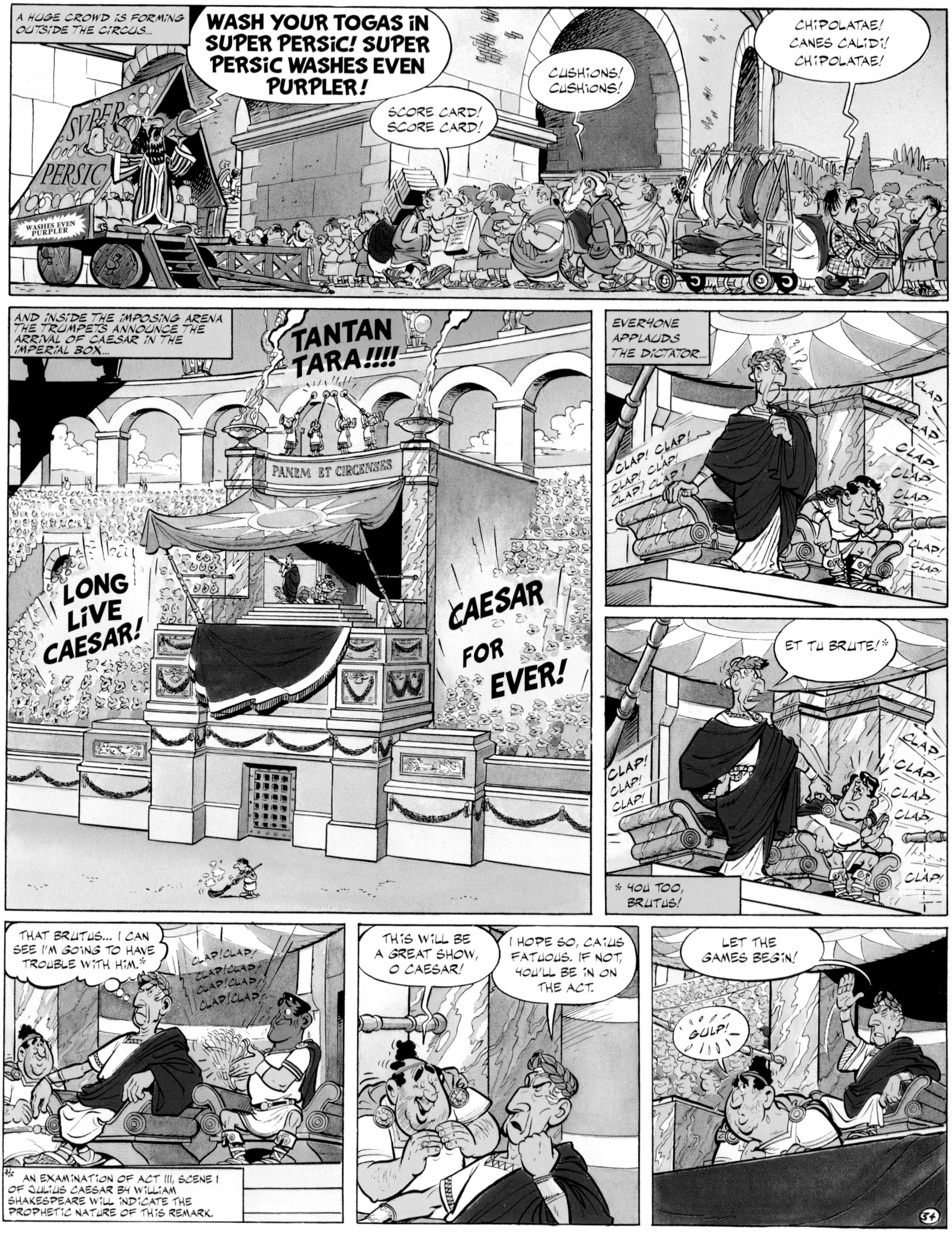

A HUGE CROWD IS FORMING OUTSIDE THE CIRCUS...
WASH YOUR TOGAS IN SUPER PERSIC! SUPER PERSIC WASHES EVEN PURPLER!
SUPER PERSIC
WASHES EVEN PURPLER
SCORE CARD! SCORE CARD!
CUSHIONS! CUSHIONS!
CHIPOLATAE! CANES CALIDI! CHIPOLATAE!
AND INSIDE THE IMPOSING ARENA THE TRUMPETS ANNOUNCE THE ARRIVAL OF CAESAR IN THE IMPERIAL BOX...
TANTAN TARA!!!!
PANEM ET CIRCENSES
LONG LIVE CAESAR!
CAESAR FOR EVER!
EVERYONE APPLAUDS THE DICTATOR...
CLAP! CLAP! CLAP! CLAP! CLAP! CLAP!
CLAP! CLAP! CLAP! CLAP! CLAP! CLAP! CLAP!
ET TU BRUTE!*
CLAP! CLAP! CLAP!
CLAP! CLAP! CLAP! CLAP! CLAP!
* YOU TOO, BRUTUS!
THAT BRUTUS... I CAN SEE I'M GOING TO HAVE TROUBLE WITH HIM.*
CLAP! CLAP! CLAP! CLAP! CLAP! CLAP! CLAP! CLAP!
* AN EXAMINATION OF ACT III, SCENE I OF JULIUS CAESAR BY WILLIAM SHAKESPEARE WILL INDICATE THE PROPHETIC NATURE OF THIS REMARK.
THIS WILL BE A GREAT SHOW, O CAESAR!
I HOPE SO, CAIUS FATUOUS. IF NOT, YOU'LL BE IN ON THE ACT.
LET THE GAMES BEGIN!
GULP!
34

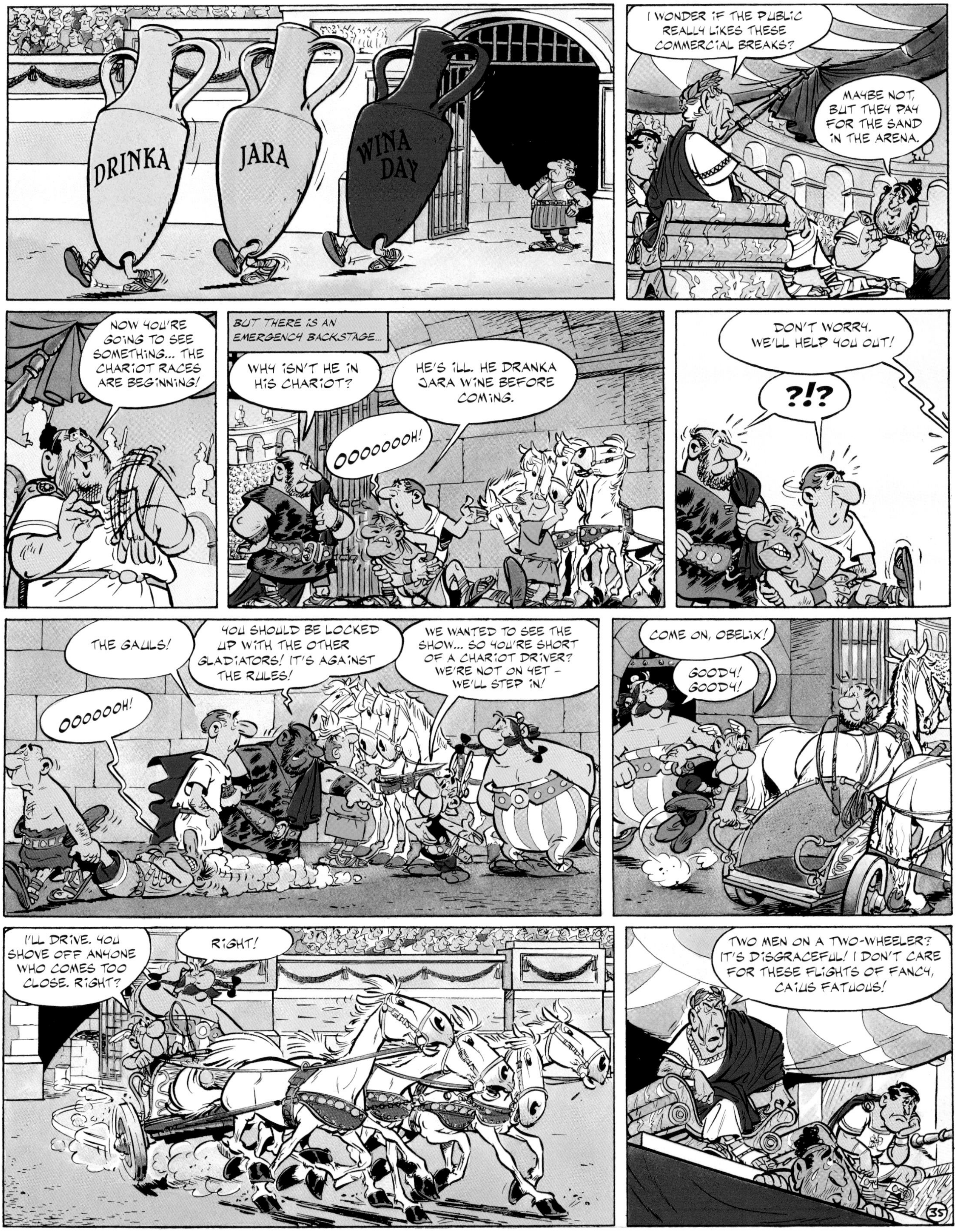
DRINKA
JARA
WINA DAY
I WONDER IF THE PUBLIC REALLY LIKES THESE COMMERCIAL BREAKS?
MAYBE NOT, BUT THEY PAY FOR THE SAND IN THE ARENA.
NOW YOU'RE GOING TO SEE SOMETHING... THE CHARIOT RACES ARE BEGINNING!
BUT THERE IS AN EMERGENCY BACKSTAGE...
WHY ISN'T HE IN HIS CHARIOT?
HE'S ILL. HE DRANKA JARA WINE BEFORE COMING.
OOOOOOOH!
DON'T WORRY. WE'LL HELP YOU OUT!
?!?
THE GAULS!
YOU SHOULD BE LOCKED UP WITH THE OTHER GLADIATORS! IT'S AGAINST THE RULES!
WE WANTED TO SEE THE SHOW... SO YOU'RE SHORT OF A CHARIOT DRIVER? WE'RE NOT ON YET – WE'LL STEP IN!
OOOOOOH!
COME ON, OBELIX!
GOODY! GOODY!
I'LL DRIVE. YOU SHOVE OFF ANYONE WHO COMES TOO CLOSE. RIGHT?
RIGHT!
TWO MEN ON A TWO-WHEELER? IT'S DISGRACEFUL! I DON'T CARE FOR THESE FLIGHTS OF FANCY, CAIUS FATUOUS!
35

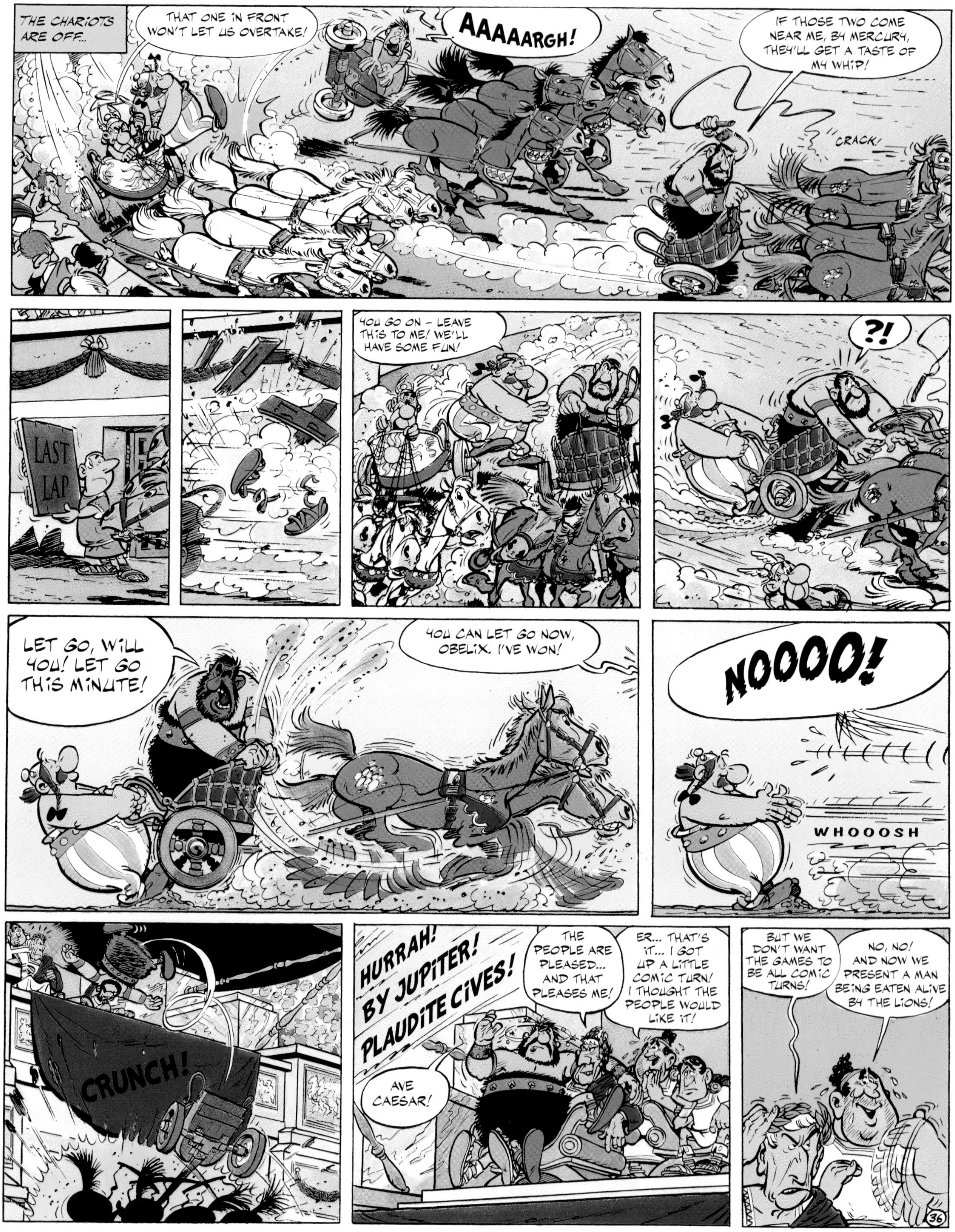

THE CHARIOTS ARE OFF...
THAT ONE IN FRONT WON'T LET US OVERTAKE!
AAAAARGH!
IF THOSE TWO COME NEAR ME, BY MERCURY, THEY'LL GET A TASTE OF MY WHIP!
CRACK!
LAST LAP
YOU GO ON – LEAVE THIS TO ME! WE'LL HAVE SOME FUN!
?!
LET GO, WILL YOU! LET GO THIS MINUTE!
YOU CAN LET GO NOW, OBELIX. I'VE WON!
NOOOO!
WHOOOSH
CRUNCH!
HURRAH!
BY JUPITER!
PLAUDITE CIVES!
AVE CAESAR!
THE PEOPLE ARE PLEASED... AND THAT PLEASES ME!
ER... THAT'S IT... I GOT UP A LITTLE COMIC TURN! I THOUGHT THE PEOPLE WOULD LIKE IT!
BUT WE DON'T WANT THE GAMES TO BE ALL COMIC TURNS!
NO, NO! AND NOW WE PRESENT A MAN BEING EATEN ALIVE BY THE LIONS!
36

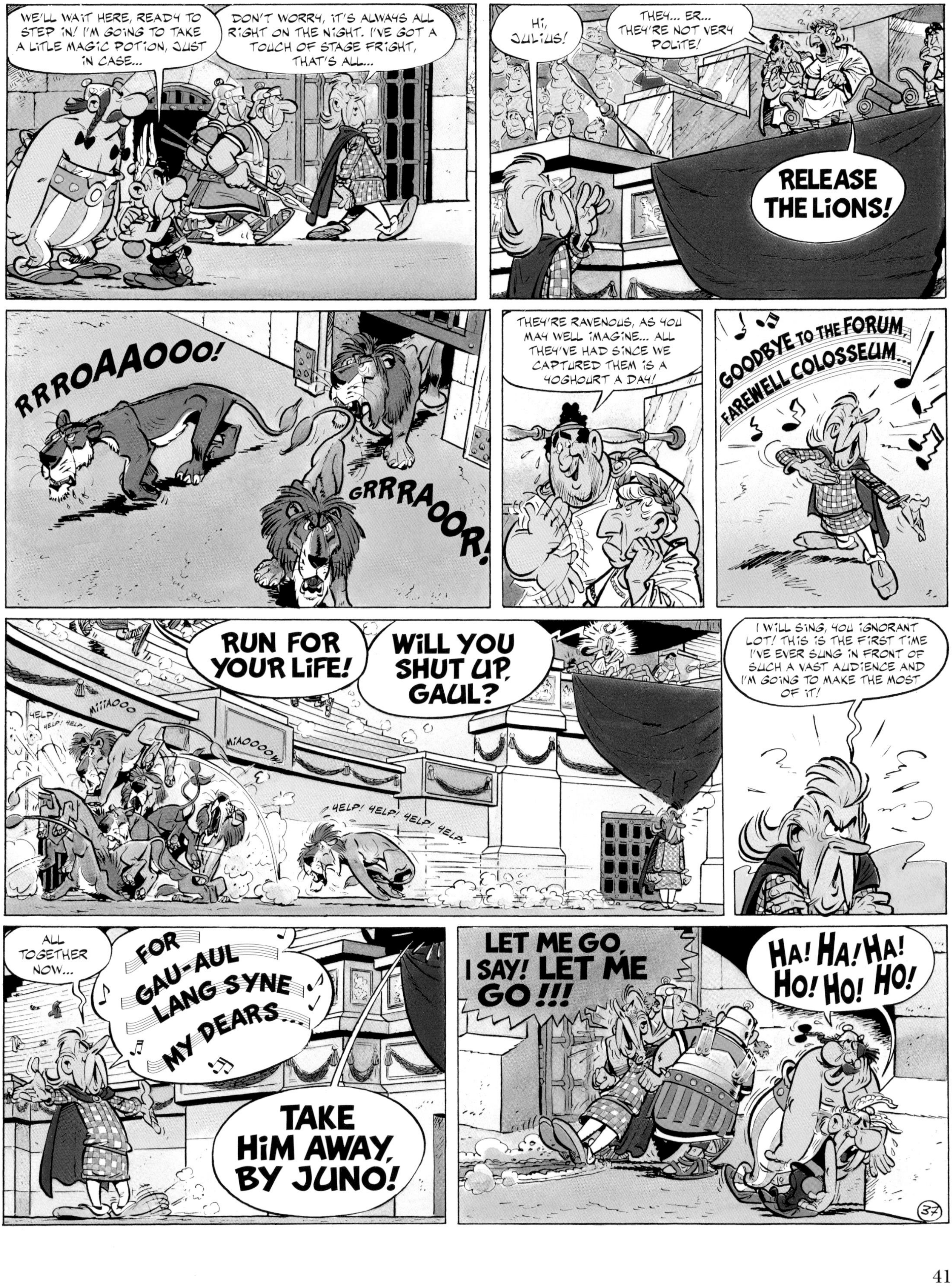
WE'LL WAIT HERE, READY TO STEP IN! I'M GOING TO TAKE A LITTLE MAGIC POTION, JUST IN CASE...
DON'T WORRY, IT'S ALWAYS ALL RIGHT ON THE NIGHT. I'VE GOT A TOUCH OF STAGE FRIGHT, THAT'S ALL...
HI, JULIUS!
THEY... ER... THEY'RE NOT VERY POLITE!
RELEASE THE LIONS!
RRROAAAOOO!
GRRRRAOOR!
THEY'RE RAVENOUS, AS YOU MAY WELL IMAGINE... ALL THEY'VE HAD SINCE WE CAPTURED THEM IS A YOGHOURT A DAY!
GOODBYE TO THE FORUM, FAREWELL COLOSSEUM...
RUN FOR YOUR LIFE!
WILL YOU SHUT UP, GAUL?
HELP! HELP! HELP!
MIIIAOOO
MIAOOOOW
HELP! HELP! HELP! HELP! HELP!
I WILL SING, YOU IGNORANT LOT! THIS IS THE FIRST TIME I'VE EVER SUNG IN FRONT OF SUCH A VAST AUDIENCE AND I'M GOING TO MAKE THE MOST OF IT!
ALL TOGETHER NOW...
FOR GAU-AUL LANG SYNE MY DEARS...
TAKE HIM AWAY, BY JUNO!
LET ME GO, I SAY! LET ME GO!!!
HA! HA! HA! HO! HO! HO!
37

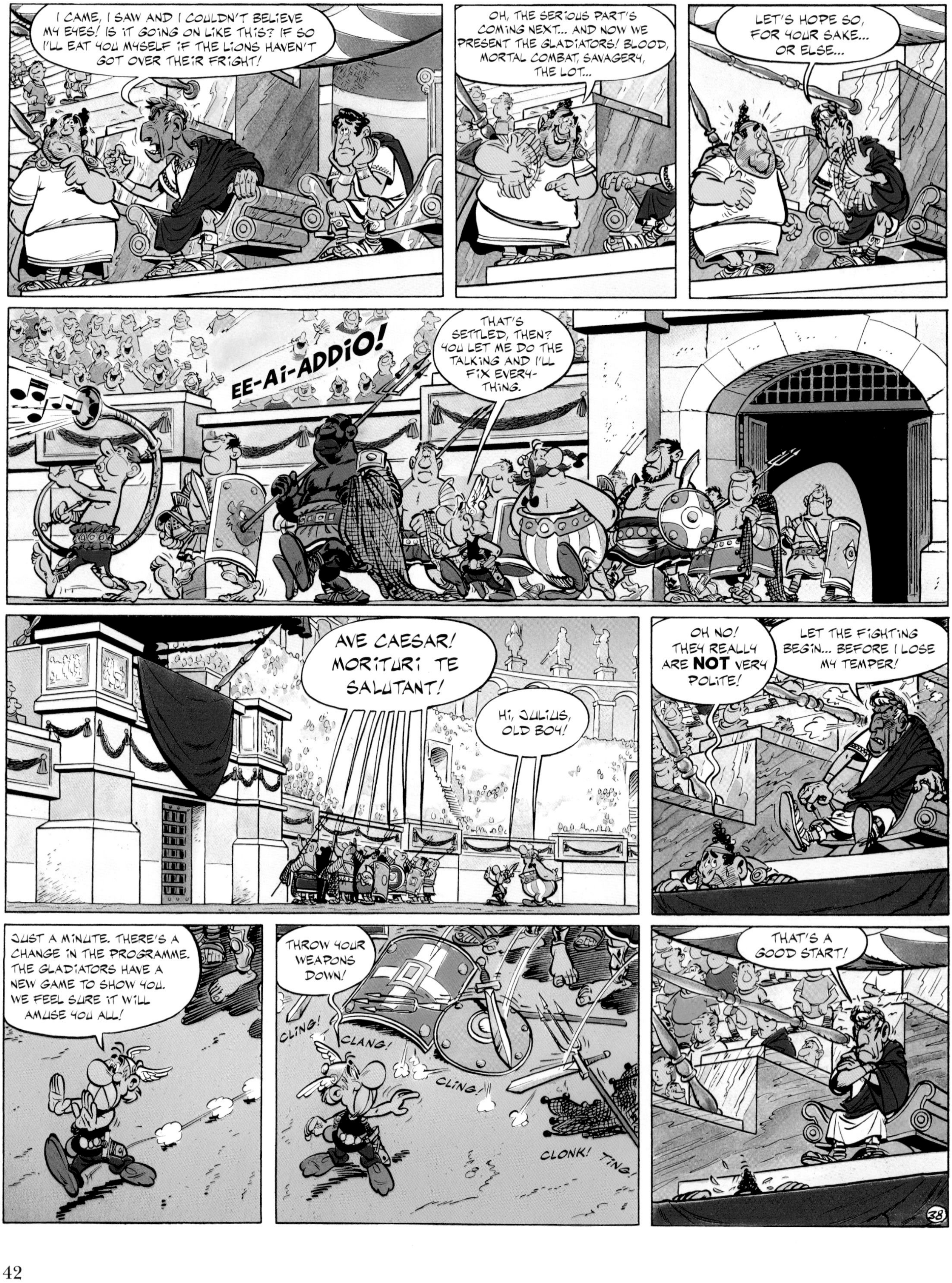

I CAME, I SAW AND I COULDN'T BELIEVE MY EYES! IS IT GOING ON LIKE THIS? IF SO I'LL EAT YOU MYSELF IF THE LIONS HAVEN'T GOT OVER THEIR FRIGHT!
OH, THE SERIOUS PART'S COMING NEXT... AND NOW WE PRESENT THE GLADIATORS! BLOOD, MORTAL COMBAT, SAVAGERY, THE LOT...
LET'S HOPE SO, FOR YOUR SAKE... OR ELSE...
EE-AI-ADDIO!
THAT'S SETTLED, THEN? YOU LET ME DO THE TALKING AND I'LL FIX EVERY-THING.
AVE CAESAR! MORITURI TE SALUTANT!
HI, JULIUS, OLD BOY!
OH NO! THEY REALLY ARE **NOT** VERY POLITE!
LET THE FIGHTING BEGIN... BEFORE I LOSE MY TEMPER!
JUST A MINUTE. THERE'S A CHANGE IN THE PROGRAMME. THE GLADIATORS HAVE A NEW GAME TO SHOW YOU. WE FEEL SURE IT WILL AMUSE YOU ALL!
THROW YOUR WEAPONS DOWN!
CLING!
CLANG!
CLING!
CLONK!
TING!
THAT'S A GOOD START!
38

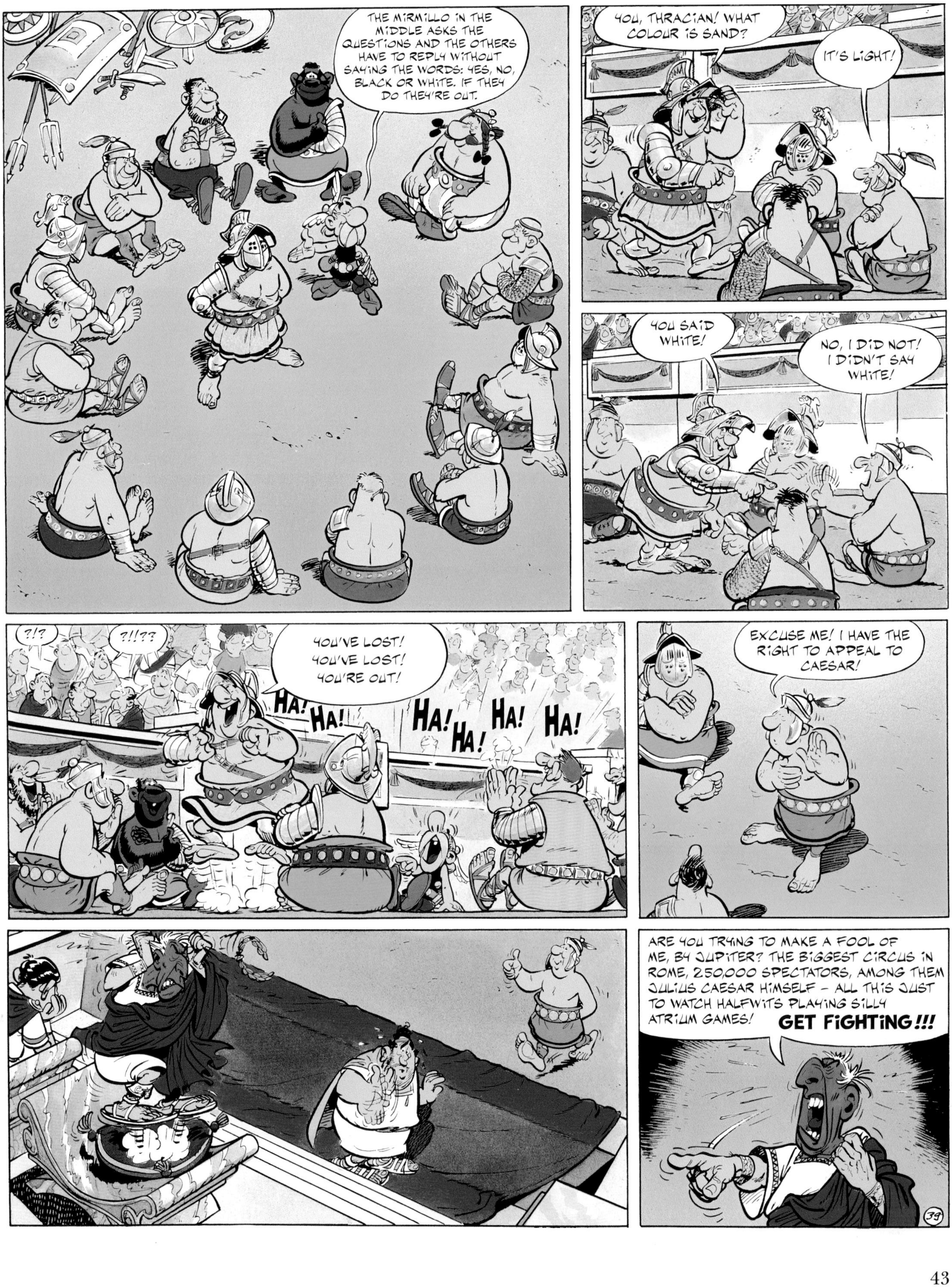
THE MIRMILLO IN THE MIDDLE ASKS THE QUESTIONS AND THE OTHERS HAVE TO REPLY WITHOUT SAYING THE WORDS: YES, NO, BLACK OR WHITE. IF THEY DO THEY'RE OUT.
YOU, THRACIAN! WHAT COLOUR IS SAND?
IT'S LIGHT!
YOU SAID WHITE!
NO, I DID NOT! I DIDN'T SAY WHITE!
?!?
?!!??
YOU'VE LOST! YOU'VE LOST! YOU'RE OUT!
HA! HA! HA! HA! HA! HA!
EXCUSE ME! I HAVE THE RIGHT TO APPEAL TO CAESAR!
ARE YOU TRYING TO MAKE A FOOL OF ME, BY JUPITER? THE BIGGEST CIRCUS IN ROME, 250,000 SPECTATORS, AMONG THEM JULIUS CAESAR HIMSELF – ALL THIS JUST TO WATCH HALFWITS PLAYING SILLY ATRIUM GAMES! GET FIGHTING!!!
39

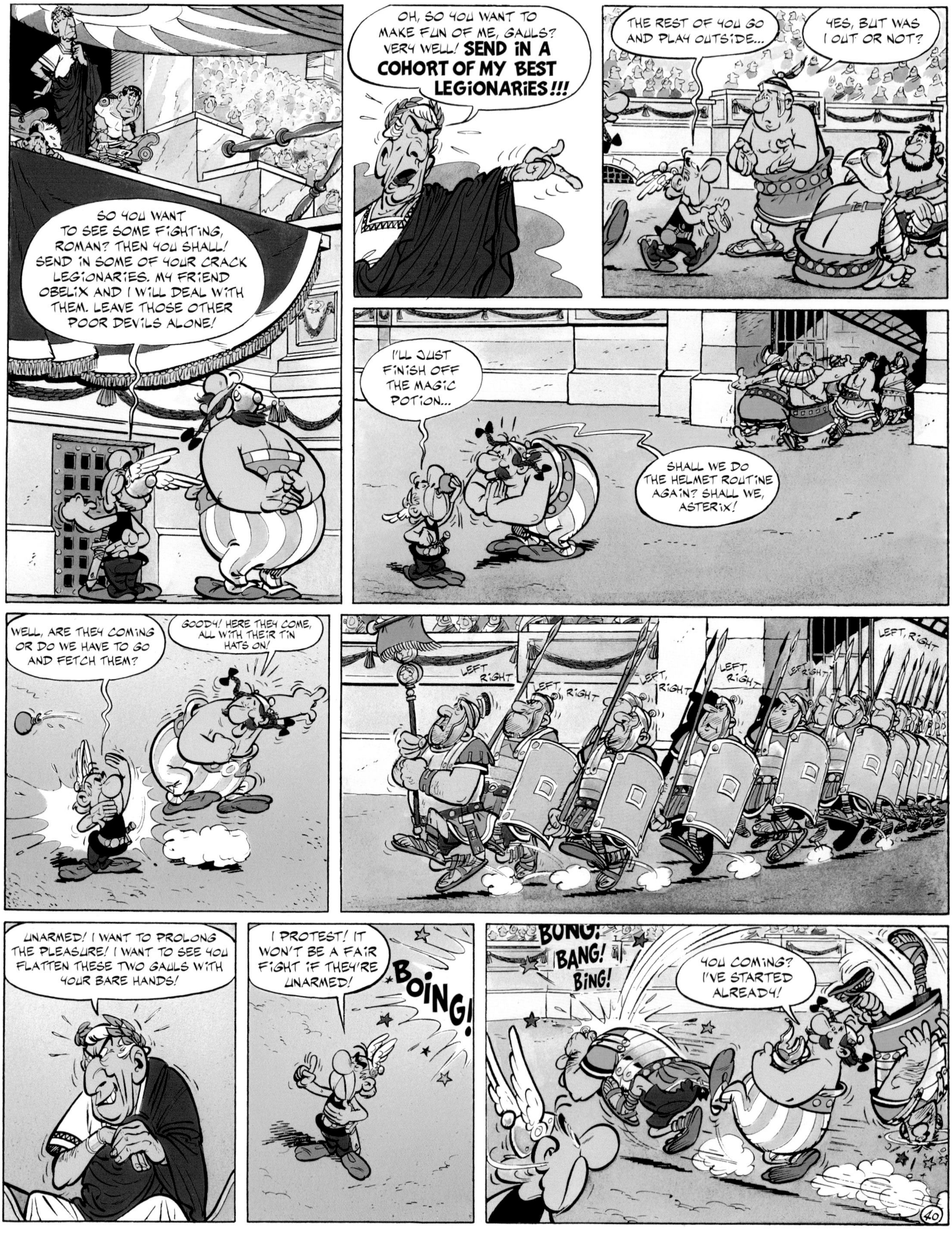
SO YOU WANT TO SEE SOME FIGHTING, ROMAN? THEN YOU SHALL! SEND IN SOME OF YOUR CRACK LEGIONARIES. MY FRIEND OBELIX AND I WILL DEAL WITH THEM. LEAVE THOSE OTHER POOR DEVILS ALONE!
OH, SO YOU WANT TO MAKE FUN OF ME, GAULS? VERY WELL! SEND IN A COHORT OF MY BEST LEGIONARIES!!!
THE REST OF YOU GO AND PLAY OUTSIDE...
YES, BUT WAS I OUT OR NOT?
I'LL JUST FINISH OFF THE MAGIC POTION...
SHALL WE DO THE HELMET ROUTINE AGAIN? SHALL WE, ASTERIX!
WELL, ARE THEY COMING OR DO WE HAVE TO GO AND FETCH THEM?
GOODY! HERE THEY COME, ALL WITH THEIR TIN HATS ON!
LEFT, RIGHT
LEFT, RIGHT
LEFT, RIGHT
LEFT, RIGHT
LEFT, RIGHT
LEFT, RIGHT
UNARMED! I WANT TO PROLONG THE PLEASURE! I WANT TO SEE YOU FLATTEN THESE TWO GAULS WITH YOUR BARE HANDS!
I PROTEST! IT WON'T BE A FAIR FIGHT IF THEY'RE UNARMED!
BOING!
BONG!
BANG!
BING!
YOU COMING? I'VE STARTED ALREADY!
40

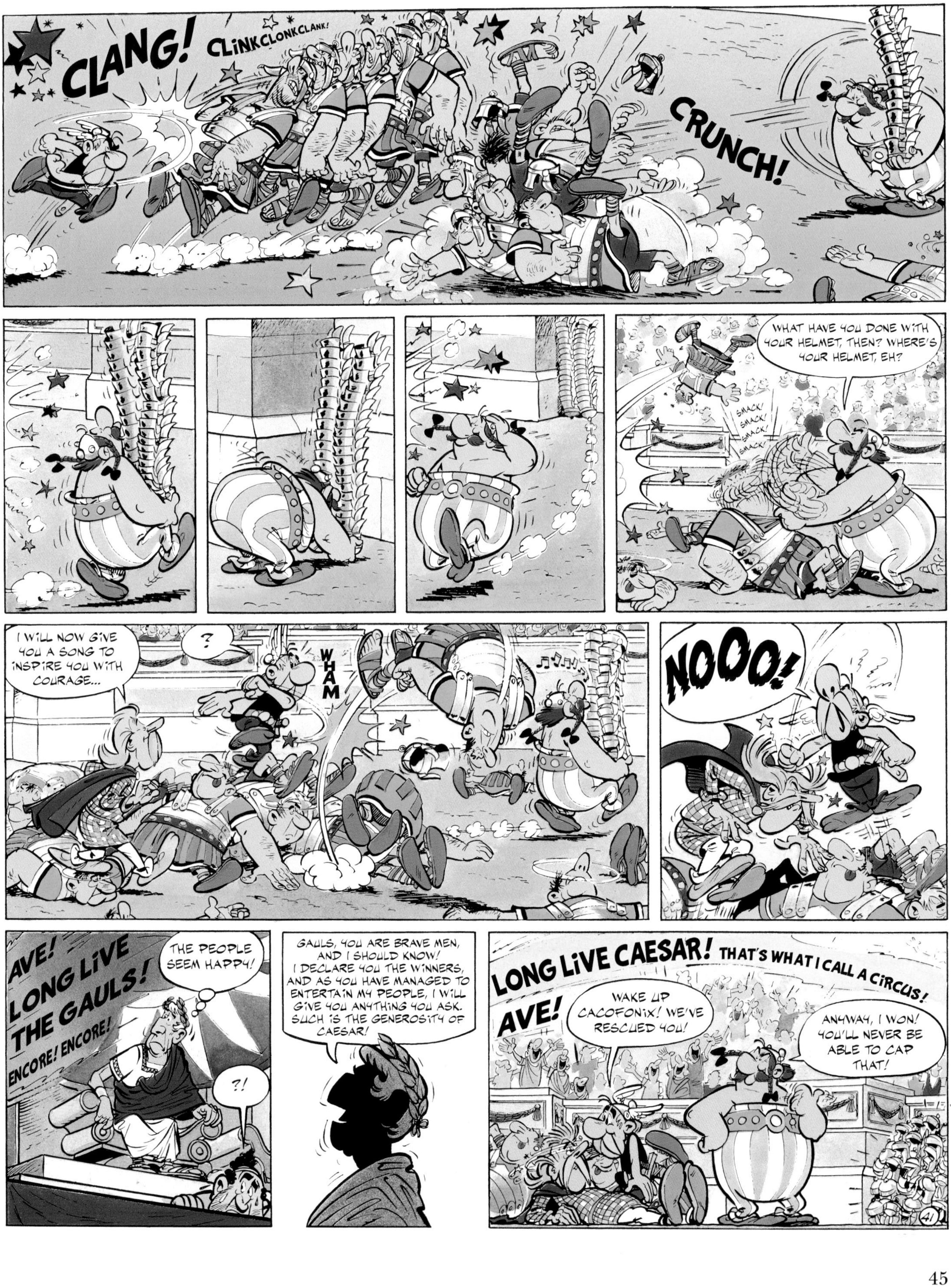
CLANG!
CLINKCLONKCLANK!
CRUNCH!
WHAT HAVE YOU DONE WITH YOUR HELMET, THEN? WHERE'S YOUR HELMET, EH?
SMACK! SMACK! SMACK! SMACK!
I WILL NOW GIVE YOU A SONG TO INSPIRE YOU WITH COURAGE...
?
WHAM
NOOO!
AVE! LONG LIVE THE GAULS! ENCORE! ENCORE!
THE PEOPLE SEEM HAPPY!
?!
GAULS, YOU ARE BRAVE MEN, AND I SHOULD KNOW! I DECLARE YOU THE WINNERS, AND AS YOU HAVE MANAGED TO ENTERTAIN MY PEOPLE, I WILL GIVE YOU ANYTHING YOU ASK. SUCH IS THE GENEROSITY OF CAESAR!
LONG LIVE CAESAR! THAT'S WHAT I CALL A CIRCUS! AVE!
WAKE UP CACOFONIX! WE'VE RESCUED YOU!
ANYWAY, I WON! YOU'LL NEVER BE ABLE TO CAP THAT!
41

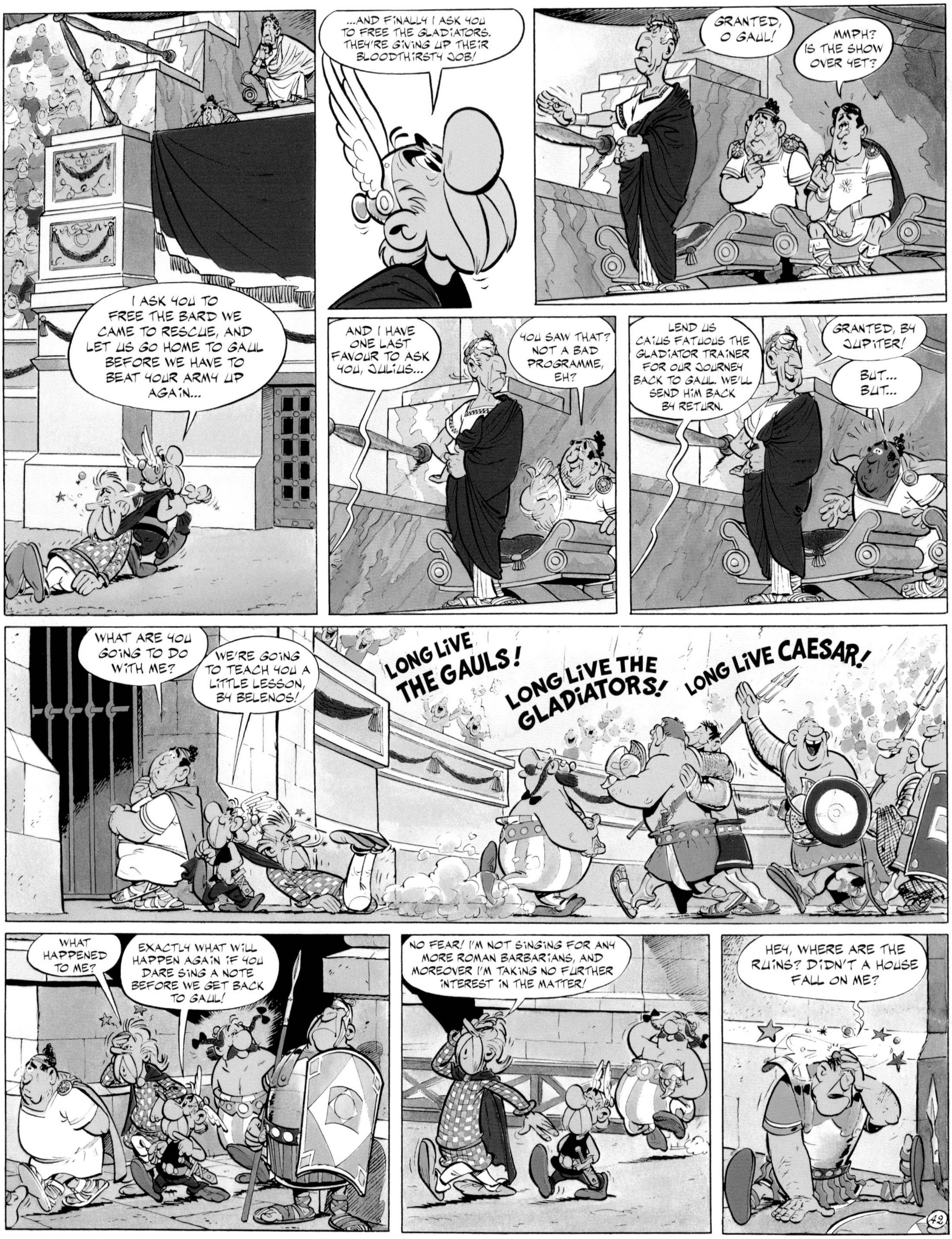
I ASK YOU TO FREE THE BARD WE CAME TO RESCUE, AND LET US GO HOME TO GAUL BEFORE WE HAVE TO BEAT YOUR ARMY UP AGAIN...
...AND FINALLY I ASK YOU TO FREE THE GLADIATORS. THEY'RE GIVING UP THEIR BLOODTHIRSTY JOB!
GRANTED, O GAUL!
MMPH? IS THE SHOW OVER YET?
AND I HAVE ONE LAST FAVOUR TO ASK YOU, JULIUS...
YOU SAW THAT? NOT A BAD PROGRAMME, EH?
LEND US CAIUS FATUOUS THE GLADIATOR TRAINER FOR OUR JOURNEY BACK TO GAUL. WE'LL SEND HIM BACK BY RETURN.
GRANTED, BY JUPITER!
BUT... BUT...
WHAT ARE YOU GOING TO DO WITH ME?
WE'RE GOING TO TEACH YOU A LITTLE LESSON, BY BELENOS!
LONG LIVE THE GAULS!
LONG LIVE THE GLADIATORS!
LONG LIVE CAESAR!
WHAT HAPPENED TO ME?
EXACTLY WHAT WILL HAPPEN AGAIN IF YOU DARE SING A NOTE BEFORE WE GET BACK TO GAUL!
NO FEAR! I'M NOT SINGING FOR ANY MORE ROMAN BARBARIANS, AND MOREOVER I'M TAKING NO FURTHER INTEREST IN THE MATTER!
HEY, WHERE ARE THE RUINS? DIDN'T A HOUSE FALL ON ME?
42

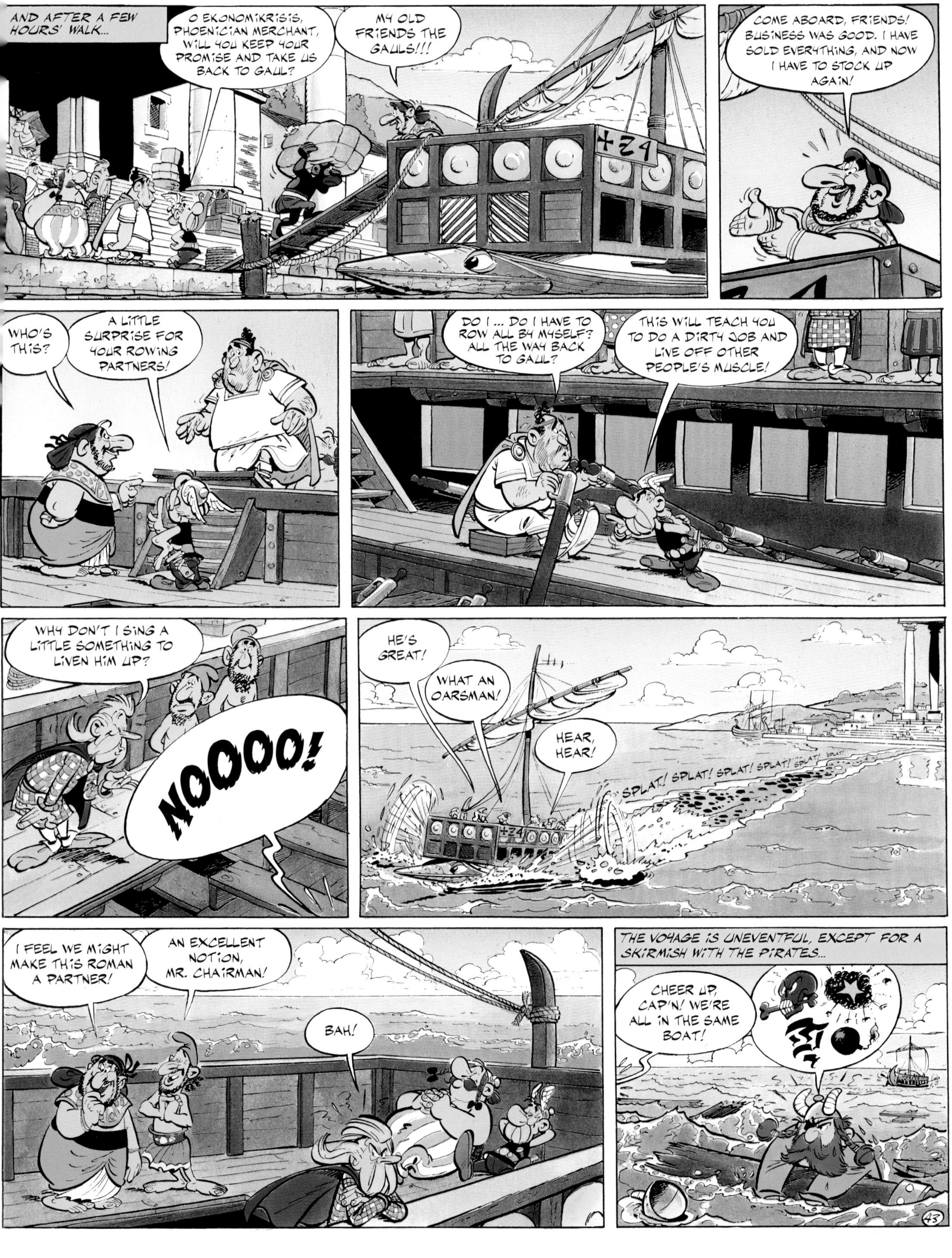
AND AFTER A FEW HOURS' WALK...
O EKONOMIKRISIS, PHOENICIAN MERCHANT, WILL YOU KEEP YOUR PROMISE AND TAKE US BACK TO GAUL?
MY OLD FRIENDS THE GAULS!!!
+Z4
COME ABOARD, FRIENDS! BUSINESS WAS GOOD. I HAVE SOLD EVERYTHING, AND NOW I HAVE TO STOCK UP AGAIN!
WHO'S THIS?
A LITTLE SURPRISE FOR YOUR ROWING PARTNERS!
DO I ... DO I HAVE TO ROW ALL BY MYSELF? ALL THE WAY BACK TO GAUL?
THIS WILL TEACH YOU TO DO A DIRTY JOB AND LIVE OFF OTHER PEOPLE'S MUSCLE!
WHY DON'T I SING A LITTLE SOMETHING TO LIVEN HIM UP?
NOOOO!
HE'S GREAT!
WHAT AN OARSMAN!
HEAR, HEAR!
SPLAT! SPLAT! SPLAT! SPLAT! SPLAT! SPLAT! SPLAT!
I FEEL WE MIGHT MAKE THIS ROMAN A PARTNER!
AN EXCELLENT NOTION, MR. CHAIRMAN!
BAH!
THE VOYAGE IS UNEVENTFUL, EXCEPT FOR A SKIRMISH WITH THE PIRATES...
CHEER UP, CAP'N! WE'RE ALL IN THE SAME BOAT!
43

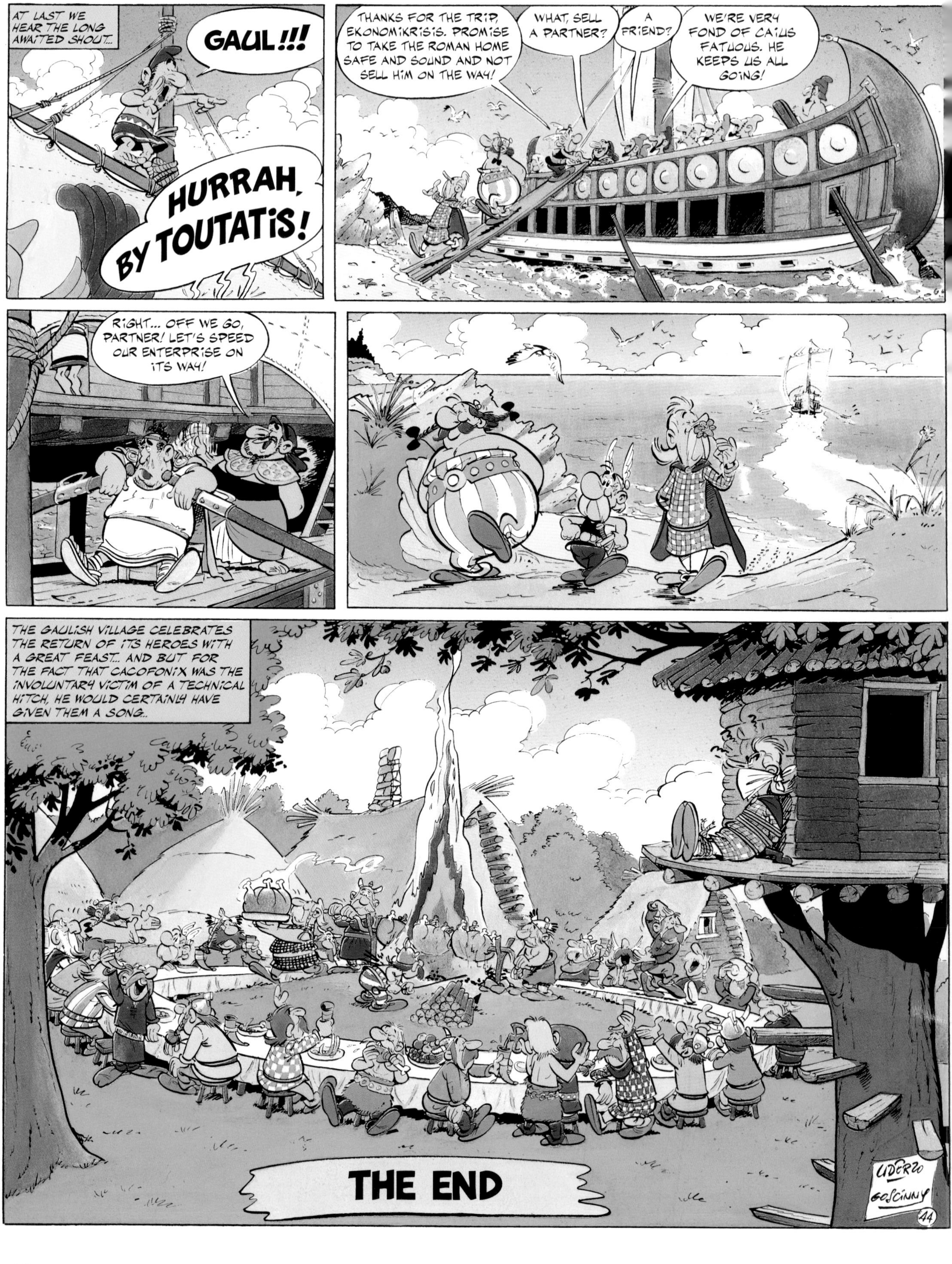
AT LAST WE HEAR THE LONG AWAITED SHOUT...
GAUL!!!
HURRAH, BY TOUTATIS!
THANKS FOR THE TRIP, EKONOMIKRISIS. PROMISE TO TAKE THE ROMAN HOME SAFE AND SOUND AND NOT SELL HIM ON THE WAY!
WHAT, SELL A PARTNER?
A FRIEND?
WE'RE VERY FOND OF CAIUS FATUOUS. HE KEEPS US ALL GOING!
RIGHT... OFF WE GO, PARTNER! LET'S SPEED OUR ENTERPRISE ON ITS WAY!
THE GAULISH VILLAGE CELEBRATES THE RETURN OF ITS HEROES WITH A GREAT FEAST... AND BUT FOR THE FACT THAT CACOFONIX WAS THE INVOLUNTARY VICTIM OF A TECHNICAL HITCH, HE WOULD CERTAINLY HAVE GIVEN THEM A SONG...
THE END
UDERZO
GOSCINNY
44

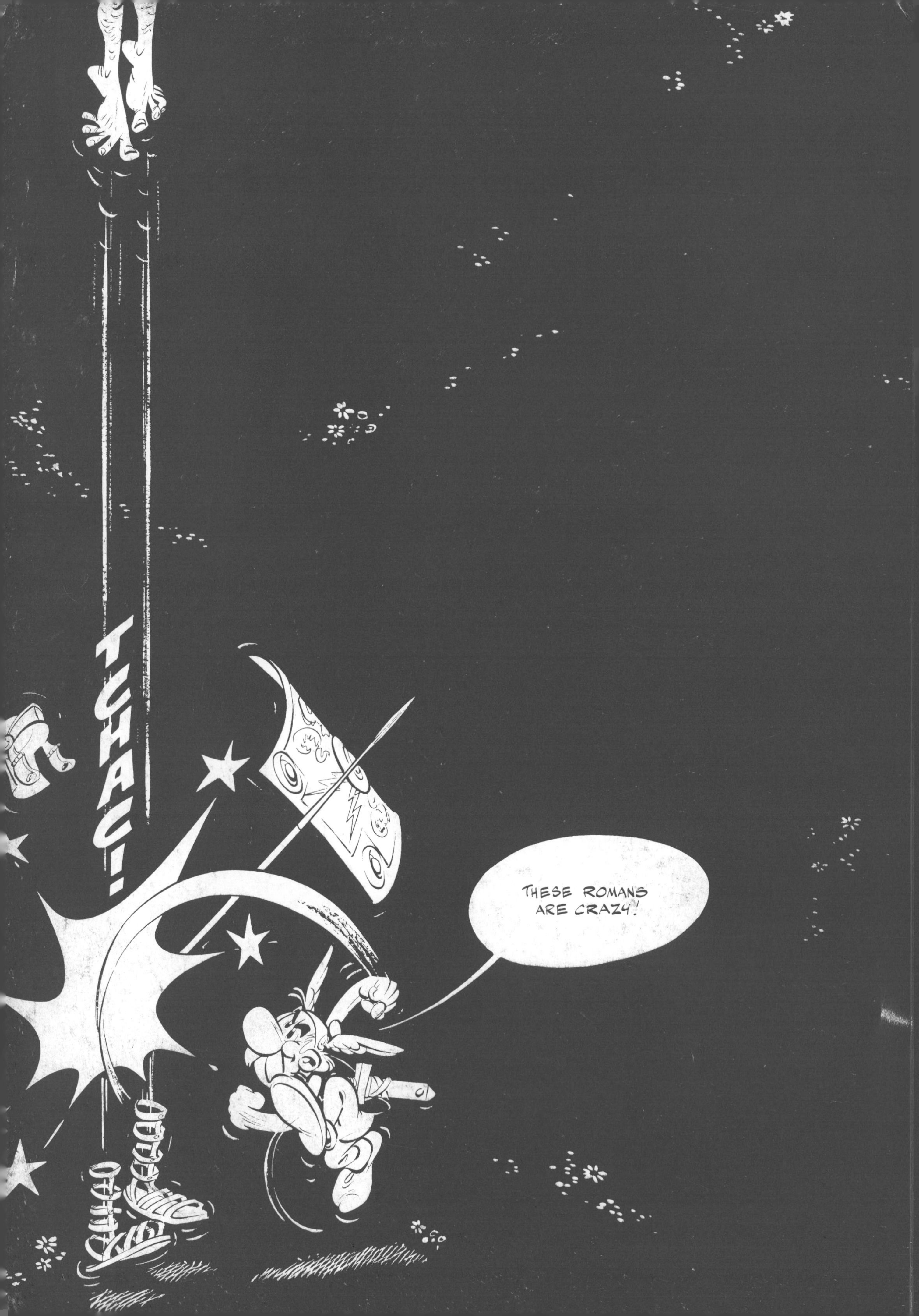
TCHAC!!
THESE ROMANS ARE CRAZY!